Read

Touchstone Se

"So good has got into my dreams and is only surpassed by Jack Finney, the master in time travel, but if this guy carries on in same vein I cannot wait..."

"An engaging time travel story, gradually demanding more concentration and weaving itself into more than simple there and back again stories."

"I ordered the whole set and was glad I did. The stories were fantastic..."

"From the first book to the last in the first season I was hooked. Some nights went to bed intending to read just a chapter or two but found myself not being able to stop reading..."

"Engrossing and never quite does what you expect..."

"Superb really enjoyed this series can't wait for more!"

Touchstone (1: The Sins of the Fathers) [1912]

"I couldn't put it down…"

"Makes for an interesting, enjoyable and easy read, and opens the reader's eyes to a time in Moseley long forgotten. It draws your attention to details of how the area was 100 years ago: the beautiful old buildings, the steam tram, how the Village green was actually green…"

"An extremely riveting short book that I didn't want to end and would have loved the book to be longer..."

"I have read a few time travel books but this one really got to me. I thought it was going to be a typical teenage romance but it certainly wasn't. Absolutely gripping…"

"I was rapt up in the story, couldn't put it down."

"I didn't expect to be so blown away as I was with this… I felt I could go and visit and really see these places. I love the characters and simply adored this book."

"Tried this out on a whim, very pleased I did, crisply written, engaging and thrilling, enjoyed it so much, I bought the series!"

"I must admit I love any books that have time travel in them, and this one didn't disappoint either. To make things even better, was to get to the end of this book knowing there were more to come. I ended up purchasing all five of the books and reading them one after the other over the space of a couple of days."

"A story to make you feel you have gone back to Birmingham in 1912. I could not put it down and can't wait to get into the next adventure."

Touchstone (2: Family at War) [1940]

"A very good short book that kept me riveted through the whole story — I never wanted it to end."

"Brings home to one what life must have been like on the

Home Front, in cities suffering nightly air raids. Doesn't flinch from the true horrors of the Blitz, nor the petty squabbles amid the rubble…"

"The historical detail in these books is fantastic, found myself wanting to know more about the area and the times."

"Initially thought it purely for children, but pleasantly surprised by the author's convincing style and obvious research into the time period concerned… all in all much better than expected, will be looking out for more by this author."

"Basically, it's a wonderful read - I just love these time travel books, whatever shape or form they have. This one was special… I believe it's one of the best series of its kind."

"Although the Touchstone books may have been written for a younger audience, I assure you; if you are a true fan of timeslip reads these will not disappoint! Each went by far too fast and I find myself waiting in anticipation for the next instalment. Rachel and Danny, along with the characters they meet on their 'journeys' are real, likable and completely caught up in the craziness that's so drastically changed their lives. Delightfully, Andy Conway has a unique way of throwing in twists and turns when least expected. For the price, you won't be better entertained, and soon, you too will be as hooked as I am."

Touchstone (3: All the Time in the World) [1966]

"I've read all three of the *Touchstone* stories now and each brings the period, in this case the sixties, to life. By concentrating on one area of the world, Moseley, Andy

Conway has given it a depth and realism. He turned my preconceptions of the swinging sixties upside down a couple of times."

"As per the previous two in this series, it is an interesting concept and is developing the story nicely with obviously more time eras to come with all the central characters and now this new introduction of some sort of monitoring team. Who are they? What is their function? I'll need to keep reading the series now I'm hooked."

"Enjoyable storyline giving a bit of an insight into people and life during these times. Some historical events creatively written."

"I really enjoyed Touchstone 1 and 2 so much that today while in Birmingham I went to Moseley village to see if the place were real. Thank you for writing the books…"

"Loved this one… I got so engrossed in it that I lost track of time completely (excuse the pun) and finished this in three to four days! Highly recommended to anyone who loves a good time travel tale."

Touchstone (4: Station at the End of Time) [1959]

"A cracking, spooky read with some great twists… oozes atmosphere, reminiscent of old TV shows like Sapphire and Steel or the Twilight Zone… As ever, it's a cracking read which never really stops for breath, exactly like the freight train bearing down on the protagonist's grandmother… also comes with a bonus short story which is a real head-wrecker."

"Best one yet. I really love this series of books and this is the most gripping yet. Although not familiar with Birmingham it is still fascinating to hear of the old Kings Heath station and the images it creates in my mind. Also take the time to read the short article at the end."

"This was a good read, enjoyed the whole series."

"Just read Touchstone 1-4 in one sitting. Unfortunately, I have now time-travelled up to your writing speed. Looking forward to Touchstone 5."

Touchstone (5: Let's Fall in Love for the Last Time) [1934]

"I've thoroughly enjoyed every bit of this series. So many twists and turns, just when I think I've sussed out what's happening, there's another twist and I was wrong. As soon as I've finished one book I instantly downloaded the next... this is an incredible story. If, like me, you love time travel novels, you'll love this."

"The plot is definitely thickening. Over the course of the five books, with the brilliant slight diversion of book 4, I have fallen deeper and deeper into the story of Rachel and Danny and the stories of the people around them."

"I am by far a *huge* fan of anything time travel related, and this series of time travel books had me hooked from book number one."

"Waited, waited, waited and waited for this. Now read it. Loved it. Can't wait for the next one. Also looking forward to the spin off sequels. Amazing story."

"What a find! I have never read anything by Andy Conway

before — but I'm now hooked! Not only was the story thoroughly enjoyable, it was also very thought provoking. Andy Conway certainly makes you think about how ordinary people lived and how their values and belief systems have changed so dramatically over the past 100 years."

Touchstone (6: Fade to Grey) [1980]

"This series has had me hooked from start to finish. I'm sad it's ended but glad it's not the end. I'm now looking forward to the next season. It's a magnificent story."

"A great series and a fine final episode, probably the best yet and by far the longest. Can't wait for series two, I am going to miss going to bed with this book at night!"

"Absolutely Superb! I have thoroughly enjoyed the whole *Touchstone* series and I have to say I've been eagerly awaiting this one, the last in the series. I wasn't disappointed in any way! If you haven't read this series yet — you simply must! Go and download *Touchstone 1. The Sins of the Fathers* — but beware — you will be hooked!!"

Buried in Time [1888]

"Inventively brilliant alternative history. Enjoyed the first Touchstone series and this is deeper, darker and more inventive."

"Everyone loves a good Jack the Ripper tale. This is one."

"Great read, and thought provoking on whom Jack the Ripper really was. Look forward to reading Touchstone series 2."

TOUCHSTONE : 1. THE SINS OF THE FATHERS

Andy Conway is the prolific novelist, screenwriter and time traveller behind the *Touchstone* series. His first feature film, *Arjun & Alison*, toured film festivals around the world and UK cinemas in 2014. His second, *An American Exorcism*, will be released in 2018.

Read more at andyconway.net

Also by Andy Conway

Touchstone Season 1
1: The Sins of the Fathers [1912]
2: Family at War [1940]
3: All the Time in the World [1966]
4: Station at the End of Time [1959]
5: Let's Fall in Love for the Last Time [1934]
6: Fade to Grey [1980]

Touchstone Season 2
Buried in Time [1888]
Bright Star Falling [1874-1887]
Bright Star Rising [1887]

Novels
Train Can't Bring Me Home
The Budapest Breakfast Club
The Striker's Fear of the Open Goal
Lovers in Paris
Long Dead Road *(with Jack Turner)*

Novellas
The Girl with the Bomb Inside
The Very Thought of You

Shorts
Meet Me in Montmartre
Ghosts on the Moor
The Reluctant Time Traveller

Non-Fiction
Punk Publishing *(with David Wake)*

Touchstone
1. The Sins of the Fathers

WALLBANK

This is a work of fiction.
Names, characters, places, and incidents either are the product of the author's imagination or are used fictitiously, and any resemblance to any persons, living or dead, business establishments, events, or locales is entirely coincidental.

This paperback edition 2018
2

First published in Great Britain by
Wallbank Books 2011
Copyright © Andy Conway 2011
The right of Andy Conway to be identified as the author of this work has been asserted by him in accordance with the Copyright, Designs and Patent Act, 1988 © Andy Conway 2011.

ISBN-10: 1725664097
ISBN-13: 978-1725664098

All rights reserved. No part of this publication may be reproduced, stored in a retrieval system, or transmitted in any form or by any means, electronic, mechanical, photocopying, recording or otherwise without the prior written permission of the publishers.

This book may not be lent, hired out, resold or otherwise disposed of by any way of trade in any form of binding or cover other than that in which it is published, without the prior consent of the publishers.

Cover design by Simon Moody at Wallbank Art.

To Norah

Note on the Second Edition

This is a complete rewrite of *Touchstone (1. The Sins of the Fathers)*, which increases the original story by 150%.

The original novellas for the first two Touchstone books were written in a rush of inspiration in 2011, quickly adapted from TV scripts, and, though successful, always seemed quite light, on plot as well as character. As the Touchstone saga grew, the books got longer, the tone darker, and it all seemed much more adult than the teen time travel adventure of these first two books. Over the years, I've looked at them and thought they just don't match the rest of the series, but also give a false impression of what's in store.

Finally, in 2018, I had an idea for how to solve this.

Alongside the original Rachel and Danny timeslip story, now sit a number of other chapters bringing in characters from later in the series. There's a sense that this is rounding off the experience, or, in the words of the fictional Arthur Conan Doyle who occasionally appears in Touchstone, 'sometimes the end of the story is also the beginning.'

Acknowledgments

Touchstone was first conceived in 2005 as a television drama serial and a good many people discussed its premise, various script drafts and contributed to its development as a novel.

Paul Woolf, a TV developer of some genius and, luckily for me, a flatmate of several years, read the earliest draft and discussed it keenly, offering many suggestions that allowed me to hone the story. Francois Gandolfi and Elisabeth Pinto were involved in the earliest attempts to develop the property as a drama series, and later Pip Piper also explored the possibilities. Two friends read early drafts and were sufficiently excited for me to pursue the story: namely screenwriter Jason Arnopp, author Jack Turner, and TV reviewer James Donaghy, all of whom offered constructive criticism and great ideas, the best of which I will always claim were my own.

Profuse thanks must also go to David Wake, who edited the second edition, and the army of Touchstone fans, without whose input and above all excitement, Touchstone would not be where it is today.

— 1 —

Rachel was back in the churchyard in an instant. The rotting smell of the place gagged her as she gasped a deep breath and ran over soft grass to the wrought-iron gates at the back of the graveyard. Stumbling down the slate slope, she heaved the gates open with all her strength.

Men loading barrels shouted as she ran past, heading for the chink of blazing light at the end of the alley.

She darted out to Moseley's village green, a busy crossroads hub of horse-drawn coaches, electric trams and elegant Edwardians promenading. She ran straight into a couple, wheeled round, shouted an apology and sprinted to her right, up the hill towards the Prince of Wales, gripping her long skirt, the heavy drag of it weighing her down. Startled Edwardians dodged out of her way, shouting admonitions she couldn't hear over the panting of her own breath.

Her lungs burned as she ran past the Prince of Wales and started the easier descent down the hill, legs slowing, growing heavy, her breath catching in her throat in desperate panic. She heard the rumble of the electric tram behind her, coming from the village green, and let out a desperate yelp, trying to quicken her steps. Another few moments and it would be too late.

The tram let out a wail that jolted her. She was so close now. It rattled alongside her, hissing, grumbling, taunting as it overtook, startled passengers watching her frantic sprint. She saw the house up ahead. Nearly there. And suddenly a bizarre scene erupted from it.

A girl ran out into the street. A young man came flying out of the house after her, as if fired from a cannon.

The tram's brakes screeched. Sparks flew up from the silver rails. The *ring-ring* of the tram bell split their ears.

An older man in a waistcoat dashed out of the house, following the couple, waving a cane.

The girl stopped, wheeled around and saw the tram bearing down on her.

The young man careened across the street to catch her.

Rachel ran towards them, panic on her face, arm outstretched, too late, and shouted, 'Don't!'

Someone screamed.

— 2 —

'Rachel!'

She shut down her laptop and grabbed her bag, doing a last quick check: phone, purse, bus pass, iPod, then a quick glance in the mirror, a ruffle of her auburn hair and she was out on the landing in a second, feet clacking on the bare floorboards.

She'd hated the lack of a stairs carpet for years, all through school, but now floorboards had become fashionable she'd stopped worrying about it, and she never saw any old school friends anyway, so there was no one to bring round and no embarrassment to feel. Her dad had painted them white, which was better than nothing.

'Do you want a lift or not?'

Martyn was at the foot of the stairs, tapping his wristwatch with a massive finger, a rugby league manager on the touchline.

'Yes!' she said, trying to sound sullen, but unable to hide her smile. Her dad was too funny for her to get away with being a sulky teenager.

'Come on then,' he said. 'Some of us have got proper work to go to.'

'Very funny, Dad.'

She clumped down the stairs in her DMs, his amused eyes

watching her, always teasing. He called back into the lounge.

'See you, Mum! We're off!'

Olive, her grandma, emerged from the front room for her goodbye kiss, turtle-slow.

'Ta ra, Nan.'

'Bye, Rachel,' she said and gripped her arm tightly, whispering low like it should be a secret from Martyn. 'Now, do you need any money to take to your Uni?'

'No, Nan. I'm fine.'

She kissed her sallow cheek, taking in the stale musk of her perfume and followed Martyn out. She had no money, but she didn't want to take her Nan's all the time. It wasn't fair.

Martyn was already in the car, a rust bucket that wasn't old enough to be fashionably retro nor new enough to be respectable. Rachel rushed through the chill November air to jump in and slam the door. Cold vinyl seat.

Olive waved them off from the doorstep, hugging herself, and they pulled out of the drive with the heater creaking, to join the slow snake of traffic.

'You know I'm only going to the village today?' she said.

'What?' Martyn clutched his chest, faking a heart attack. 'If I'd known that I'd have made you walk.'

'I'm late, though,' she laughed.

'You'll get fat.'

'Dad!' She grinned and punched his arm.

'All right, attacking the driver. Where's that ejector seat button?'

They were there in ten minutes – he was right, she could have walked it in five – the rush hour traffic crawling through Moseley, down St Mary's Row to the church standing sentinel over the village green. She undid her seat belt and picked up the canvas bag between her feet.

'Have a nice day with your posh University friends,' Martyn joked.

'They're not my friends,' she said. 'They're all rich kids. I hate them.'

'Do you need any money?' he said, suddenly serious.

'No. I'm fine. You're worse than Nan.'

She kissed him on his sandpaper cheek and climbed out, waving to him as he drove on through the crossroads. She waited for the lights to turn red so the traffic would stop and she could cross the road. It was busy and she could see the crowd of people already gathered on the 'village green'.

It hadn't been a village green for maybe a hundred years or more, but everyone still called it 'Moseley village' and they still called the triangular island to the side of the crossroads 'the green', which was an historical hangover she found fascinating. An idea for an essay, she thought. How the past clung so persistently to the present, and how it was exemplified in this inner city urban 'village'. Something along those lines. The thrill of study fluttered in her belly. This was the difference between school and University – a new world of independent enquiry was opening up before her; a means by which she might pursue ideas and forge an identity. To research and cogitate and forge a unique way of looking at the world that was entirely her own; that was the most exciting thing in the world right now.

The lights changed, the traffic stopped and she took a deep breath and crossed over, clutching her bag strap tightly to hide her nervousness. She'd been at University for three weeks now and even though she was the girl who'd lived locally all her life, they made her feel like she was the stranger.

She had seen old photographs of when it really had been a green, but it was paved now and contained a few benches, flowerbeds, the bus stop that led back to her house, low railings that had been put up a few years ago and now had dead flowers hanging from them to mark a road accident. The sad commemoration of someone forgotten. The village green surrounded by shops and busy morning traffic. She tried to imagine what it would have been like in the old days, when it was a peaceful little island at the centre of a real village, horses and carriages the only traffic.

The other students were waiting in clusters here and there, the groups that had already formed, and to none of which she belonged, all smoking and trying to look too cool for school. She didn't get that at all. It was University. No one had made them take a degree in History so why the pretence that it was so deadly dull and beneath them?

She stood on her own and tried not to look at the group close by dressed like rock stars, the biggest bunch of posers on the course: Jessica, Stacy, Tyrone... and Danny. He was different to the others, she could tell. He didn't dress quite as ridiculously as they did, but he was the undisputed ringleader of their sect. He wasn't as crass as them — there were deeper layers to him, and he was the only one who'd ever looked at her and actually seemed to notice her. They hadn't talked, not outside of vague platitudes when thrown together to discuss something in a seminar group, which was rare because his clique of friends usually made sure they were the only ones on their table. But Rachel thought she had a sense for what was inside people and he wasn't anywhere near as much of a freak as his friends.

She stood alone in her Primark best and wondered if the laughter that had just crackled between them was about her. She shrunk in on herself and scowled.

Her eyes fell on the upper storey of the bar on the corner. Its modern frontage curved the south-eastern corner of the village crossroads, and the name had changed several times recently. It seemed one of those bars that could never quite establish itself. Above the ground floor wooden panelled frontage that screamed cool, modern interior, the Baroque Revival of the original building looked over the village, an ornate stucco rosette, balustered battlements and latticed oriel windows.

Her favourite building in the village because, if you

squinted to shut out the ground floor, it looked like a ruined castle.

A shadow in the window up there.

A shudder passed through her. Someone walked over her grave, a ringing in her ears that blocked out the roar of the rush hour traffic for a moment. She palmed her ear till it popped, and shivered again.

Mr Fenwick arrived and they gravitated towards him. He must have parked his car nearby. He looked stupidly cheerful in the face of their sullen glares and she forced herself to stop scowling and smile so she wouldn't look like the rest of them. He was a good lecturer with a sharp sense of humour and must have been slightly younger than her dad but more handsome.

'Good morning, historians,' he shouted as they gathered round him. 'Welcome to our first field trip in the neighbourhood of Moseley. In particular, St Mary's church round the corner. Let's go.'

He headed off up the road, stepping off the green and walking up St Mary's Row past the Bull's Head pub. They followed in his wake, and turned into the churchyard further up at the lychgate entrance where the winos usually hung out.

The churchyard had a small front apron above the road where tombstones watched over the traffic below, but the main graveyard was round the rear of the church, an impressive 15th Century structure with a crenellated tower. She realized she'd never been inside it, even though she'd always liked the look of it and the way the battlements of its tower peeped over the Bull's Head pub and could be seen from the green.

They huddled around Mr Fenwick on a patch of broken, buckled paving stones and she took up position on the fringe of the crowd.

'St Mary's church has been here since the fifteenth century, five hundred years before Moseley even became a part of Birmingham, which was when, Jessica?'

Jessica looked as surprised as her ridiculous hair for a second, then shrugged and said, 'I've no idea.'

'Anyone?'

They shuffled uneasily. Jessica and Stacy smirked. Rachel's eyes fell on Danny. He caught her staring and she looked at her shoes and then at Fenwick.

'We did this a week ago,' he said. 'Danny. Is your memory any better than Jessica's?'

'Yeah,' said Danny. 'She's thick.'

Jessica punched him and Rachel stole another glance.

'So, when did this fine little suburb defect to the sprawling Birmingham metropolis?'

'1912?' said Danny.

'Wrong. Rachel, you're local, you should know?'

She looked up, surprised, and thought *it's okay to know the answer, this is Uni, not school.*

'1911?'

'Now who's the thick one, Danny Pearce?'

Everyone laughed. Mr Fenwick indicated the street they overlooked. 'Now, you all know Moseley for its fine selection of trendy bars. But we've got a pub called the Village, a fish and chip shop called the Village, and everyone calls the centre of Moseley *the Village*. Why is that?'

Danny piped up. 'Is it because it used to be a village?'

'Give him his degree right now! Yes, Danny, Moseley used to be a village. A village built around this fine mediaeval church.'

'Did it used to be all fields round here, Nick?'

Everyone laughed again and Danny smiled at his own joke. Tyrone decided to join in. He always did whatever Danny did and thought it made him just as witty.

'Do you remember it back then, Nick?'

Mr Fenwick's eyes sparkled, encouraging their banter. 'Yes, yes, very funny. Now, long before all the trendy bars opened, Moseley was a tiny village, and some of its villagers would have been buried in this churchyard. Their gravestones are long gone, but some of them remain. Look at your feet.'

They looked down and saw that the path was made of broken gravestones. A general 'Ewwwww!' went up. Rachel found herself reading the tip of someone's headstone, between her Primark shoes. *Arabella Palmer, who departed this life August 16th 1876.* Her age had been underneath, but the stone was broken off at that point and she could only make out the word *YEARS* and the top of the number. It could have been 8, or 38. She hoped it was the latter.

Mr Fenwick led them round to the rear of the church and the overgrown graveyard. Moss covered headstones leaned at various angles, some broken. Bushes and weeds had reclaimed the scarcely visible paths. There were some impressive monuments with sculpted angels and readable inscriptions, but most had faded with age. Some wealthy people had been buried here, but no one for a very long time. It was a neglected inner-city museum that few people visited except for winos and bored school kids and History students on field trips.

'Luckily for us,' he shouted, 'the graves that still exist here are from the last hundred and fifty years. That means they're all people who lived in Moseley when it was a heavily populated satellite of Birmingham. We can find out lots of things about them in the city archives and it will all be deeply fascinating and turn you into semi-professional local historians. So, I want you to choose a project partner…'

They started pairing off noisily. Rachel glanced around in panic, knowing no one was going to pick her.

'…pick a name off a gravestone. That person is going to be the subject of your local history research. Danny, come here.'

Danny sloped over to him.

'You can partner Rachel for your project. Maybe she'll

knock some sense into you.'

Rachel looked up at Danny with a hesitant smile, just in time to see Jessica shoot her a vicious look.

Danny slumped off, hands in pockets. Everyone spread out and Rachel followed Danny down to the bottom end of the cemetery, close to the green wrought-iron gates that fenced off the graveyard from a back alley that led right back to the village green.

— 3 —

Danny found himself drawn to a gravestone shaped like a small bench or a baby's cot; its edges blurred by time, the inscription faded.

Rachel joined him and sat on it, trying to decipher the words that had been chiselled in over a century ago.

'I'm not sure if it's Rees or Reed,' she said. 'It's practically worn away. Maybe it's Read, with an A.'

Danny sat behind her, not paying attention, leaning back, his hands absently roaming the surface of the gravestone.

'Listen,' he said. 'I've got an evil hangover, so can you just sort it out yourself and not bother me with it?'

'We're supposed to do this project together,' she snapped.

'We will,' he said. 'But if you could just get the name, I'd be very grateful.'

She turned away, choosing to be all offended about it, not realising how much it was hurting his head just to be out in the light. It was just his luck to get paired with some loser who wanted to turn it into a PhD.

'You and that lot over there think everything's here for your own personal amusement,' she said. 'Well, I don't a give a toss. I think you're all a bunch of—'

He didn't hear the end of her sentence. His fingers touched something warm and her voice sounded like it was coming through a tin funnel, then his ears blocked like he'd fallen underwater.

He looked over, surprised, thinking she was playing a joke. But Rachel wasn't there.

The shock was so instant that he didn't notice what would strike him every time afterwards: the noise. It was as if the constant hum of traffic that was always there wherever you were in the city had been ripped away. It was like your ears suddenly blocking while you were flying, so you had to swallow to pop them clear again.

'You shouldn't sit there. It's someone's grave.'

He looked up into the clear green eyes of a young woman.

'Hello, I'm Amy Parker. Who are you?'

She held out her hand and he shook it and wondered why he couldn't move his feet or take his eyes off hers.

'I'm... Danny,' he croaked. 'Danny Pearce.'

'And where do you live, Danny Pearce?'

'Er, Chantry Road.'

'I'm sure you don't,' she said.

There was something not right about this at all. He flexed his jaw to make his ear pop, but nothing happened. He had the sickly sensation of being trapped in a bell jar, hypnotized by her eyes.

'What?' he managed to say.

'I live at number twelve, Alcester Road and I know most of the families on Chantry Road and I've never heard of you before.'

A voice barked from the other end of the graveyard and the slightly unusual became utterly weird.

'Amy!'

Fear flashed in her green eyes. 'I have to go, Danny Pearce.'

Danny looked away from her eyes for the first time and it overloaded his senses, so many things in a sudden breathless rush, like a TV info burst, most of the details of which he would only remember later.

He saw that Amy was dressed in a black gown of the type that any middle-class girl attending a funeral circa 1912 might wear. A bearded man marched towards him dressed in a frock coat and a top hat, brandishing a cane, wide-eyed and angry, a speck of spittle at the corner of his mouth. A cluster of people around a grave in the distance, dressed in Bible black, top hats and veils. A priest in a flowing white smock that billowed in the breeze. The graveyard was not overgrown, the lawns were well kempt, the stones were not tilted and weathered but many were bright and new.

He slumped back on the gravestone, shock and panic overloading his senses.

The man grabbed Amy's arm. 'Who is he?' he barked. 'Is this the one?'

'Please, not here, Father,' she whimpered, casting a cautious glance back at the mourners in the distance.

Danny's fingers groped the surface of the gravestone as he gasped, struggling for air, hyperventilating.

The man turned, hissing spittle, brandishing his cane.

Danny knew he had to run, or have his face smashed in, but he couldn't move, frozen, like in a bad dream.

'Is he the one?'

Danny's fingers edged towards the same spot he'd touched before.

'Father! Stop it!' Amy hissed.

Mr Parker glared back at her and shoved her away. But when he turned back, Danny was gone.

— 4 —

Mr Fenwick was close to the north-eastern corner of the church, squatting by a gravestone, admiring the subtle filigreed stonework and wondering how seriously this current crop of students would be taking their task.

In every year there were a couple of standout exceptional students you knew would get Firsts from day one. These were the ones you had to feed with steady praise, but not too much in case they suffered vertigo and burned out.

Unfortunately, the broad mass of students had no academic skills or inclinations whatsoever and would remain like that for three years, if they didn't drop out. You just had to bully them constantly into the whole concept of research, analysis, discussion and referencing of primary and secondary sources.

For some this proved an impossible thing to grasp, even after three years, mainly because they seemed quite content to make no effort at all and cruise through to get a Third because it was a degree, after all. If they scraped a 2:2 they'd feel they'd performed an amazing con trick on the educational system. There were only a handful of students in every annual intake that could surprise you by going either way; displaying enough talent that they could make a serious, late burst for a First, or fail at the end and sink into a 2:1 or worse.

What was surprising was how few surprises there were.

Rachel, the one student in this year's intake he knew without a doubt would get a First, approached him and coughed shyly.

'Er… Nick,' she said.

He grinned before turning to her. It was always funny to see which students had most difficulty shaking off school and realising they could call tutors by their first name now.

'Rachel,' he said.

'We've got one. I can't work out if it's Rees or Read, but the date of death is definite. I don't know where Danny's gone, though.'

Nick squinted in the low winter sun, looking over her shoulder.

'He's over there.'

Rachel turned back to look at their gravestone twenty yards away and frowned.

Danny was sitting right there.

— 5 —

Rachel stormed back over to find Danny breathing hard, staring around him, bewildered.

'I suppose you sloped off for a fag or something. Well, I've done it now so if you don't like it, tough.'

She froze. There was something wrong. She could read it in him immediately in the way you just *know*. He looked like his hangover had turned into a full-blown panic attack.

'Are you all right?'

'No.'

'What is it?' she said.

'You won't believe what just happened.'

'What?'

Danny gulped, caught his breath, stammered. His face was white but he breathed like he'd just run twenty times around the churchyard.

'I was sitting here and you were talking and then, bam, you were gone, and I was here and it was all different and there was this girl and her father in Edwardian clothes and a funeral.'

He shook his head, like he didn't believe it himself.

'Have you been smoking?' she said.

'It was real. I was there. I talked to her.'

'What are you on about?'

'When I touched the stone,' he said. 'I went back there.'

This was weird. He was acting like a freak, which threw her, because Danny was one of the cool kids and it was really *her* job to act like a freak.

'Where?'

'I don't know. The past or something.'

'Yeah right. Whatever.'

'It's true. It was a very weird and totally lucid timeslip moment.' He pointed to the spot on the stone. 'So weird. Right there. Touch it yourself.'

She hesitated, frowning, thinking this was all going to be a joke at her expense. She glanced around. His friends were at the far end of the graveyard, lounging on a gravestone, smoking, making no attempt to research anything. No one was filming her on their phone. If it was a joke, what was the point of it? She looked back at him. His face was pale, beads of sweat on his forehead. He looked like he was about to chuck up his breakfast at any second. He wasn't joking.

She took a step towards him, leaned across, her fingers reaching uncertainly for the spot on the gravestone he was pointing to, his index finger shaking.

'Okay, let's all go this way!'

Mr Fenwick was leading the whole class towards them. She snatched her hand back and looked at Danny's face again, expecting to see a broad grin there, an amused glint in his blue eyes, but he wasn't looking at her; he was looking at the floor, embarrassed, confused.

Mr Fenwick passed by and headed for the wrought-iron gate, the other students dawdling in his wake.

'We came in the normal way but there's a little secret back here,' he called out.

He walked down the slate slope and pushed the gate open. The class filed out into the alley between the shops. Rachel followed Danny, looking back once more at the gravestone.

Mr Fenwick's voice echoed out on the alley walls as he

strode onwards. 'This used to be a wide yard, before the Barclays Bank was built in the 1920s. But if we walk down here we end up...'

They all emerged back out at the village 'green', between a chip shop and a bank.

'Back in Moseley village,' he said, as if he'd pulled a rabbit out of a hat. 'So, armed with your person from the past, let's go back to our dusty old lecture room and learn about all the various kinds of research at our disposal. Field trip over. Minibus this way.'

He headed across the green, off to the car park behind the south-eastern corner of the village crossroads.

Rachel glanced involuntarily at the latticed windows of that crumbling, ornate stucco upper floor again. As the students snaked after him, Rachel grabbed Danny's arm.

'What happened?' she whispered.

He looked over at his friends, worried, and snapped with sudden venom.

'Nothing happened, right?'

She gripped his arm harder and said with total sincerity, 'I believe you.'

He stopped, glanced at the others again.

'If you tell anyone. I'll—'

'I won't tell anyone if you don't,' she said. She gripped his arm suddenly and hissed, 'Let's come back. Tonight.'

He thought about it, working out if he could trust her. 'Okay,' he said, as if he didn't believe it himself anymore. 'Six o'clock.'

They walked on, following the others, swallowed in the full sweep of Moseley village, the pedestrian throng, cars tearing this way and that, the buses sailing through the village crossroads, and beyond it, a cityscape of office blocks on the skyline.

— 6 —

Amy Parker hissed, 'Father! Stop it!' and pulled on his arm. This was a scene. He was about to let The Secret out into the open, for all to see.

He glared at her with such hate and shoved her aside. She stumbled and twisted her ankle, falling to the soft grass with a bump.

The boy called Danny Pearce was gone and father was glancing around like a cat that had lost a mouse. The strange boy had been sitting on the gravestone, right there, a few seconds ago, and now he wasn't.

She sprang to her feet and rushed to the gravestone. He hadn't fallen off it. He wasn't lying in the grass on the other side. He wasn't down there in the back alley. The wrought-iron gates hadn't been opened and no one could have run there and vaulted the gate in five seconds. He hadn't run up the path either. The mourners gathered around poor Mr Rieper's grave were still clustered there, one or two looking back to see what the shouting was about.

'Was he the one?' her father croaked.

The anger had left him. He staggered and was about to fall so she guided him to the gravestone, where he sat with a groan. A few moments ago he had spat hate in her face, but now he was whimpering. He took his red handkerchief from his breast pocket and dabbed the spittle from his lips.

'He disappeared.'

'Yes, father. He must have run away. You scared him so.'

'Like a spirit. Like a will-o-the-wisp.'

Amy checked all around again, expecting Danny Pearce to jump out, laughing to surprise, like a boy would, always playing tricks and trying to best one.

'He ran away, father. I saw him,' she lied.

'Oh,' her father said, as if he'd somehow missed it. 'Did you?'

He was like a bewildered child. She knew it wouldn't last. Later would come shouting and raging. It always did.

'Everything all right, eh?'

A man had peeled off from the funeral, in sombre black and top hat, like the other Freemason friends of the deceased.

'Everything's fine, Mr Harper,' Amy blurted.

'You don't look so well, Richard.' Mr Harper put his hand on her father's shoulder. 'You look like you've taken a turn, old friend.'

'Father tripped on the path, Mr Harper. He'll be fine in a moment. I should get him home.'

Her father looked through Harper. Didn't recognize him. But then suddenly said, 'Reginald. What are *you* doing here?'

Mr Harper blushed and didn't know what to say. 'I came for Rieper's funeral, like you, Richard.'

'Well, I know that!' Parker snapped.

He could turn like that, in an instant, and now Mr Harper had seen it. The Secret was out. All of Moseley would know soon and point and laugh, or worse – cross the road to avoid. They would take her father away and put her in an orphanage.

'Let's get you home, Richard.'

'He's quite all right, Mr Harper. He didn't have breakfast this morning, even though I warned him he'd need it, and he had a little dizzy spell. He felt a bit under the weather this morning and wouldn't eat, you see. I warned you, didn't I, father?'

She pulled him to his feet and wiped his mouth, stuffed his handkerchief back in his pocket. Playing the mother, because there was no mother. *Don't let them see that you're playing the adult for father too.*

'Oh, I see,' said Mr Harper, more jovially. 'You should have listened to your daughter here, Richard.'

'I'll get him right home and give him some soup, Mr Harper.'

'You're a good girl, Amy.'

She pulled her father away, towards the wrought-iron gate at the rear of the churchyard. They could sneak out the back and avoid a scene. Her father's Freemason friends might not notice his absence and, perhaps, Mr Harper would say nothing. They were a secretive lot, so perhaps it wouldn't be all over Moseley.

The gates squealed as she pushed a gap for them to squeeze through. Mr Harper watched them go, smiling faintly. She walked her father down the dank yard space behind the billboards, bordering the Bull's Head. It stank of dead things. Was it the bodies they buried here, their stench coming up through the flagstones, or might it have been rotting slops from the pub?

'You're not a good girl,' her father said. 'I saw you, talking to that boy. I'll punish you for that.'

Amy whimpered and pushed her father on. He was too weak to beat her here.

The village green was crowded with too much life. She walked her father past the newsman's stand, a fake smile on her face. *We are promenading on a lovely afternoon in Moseley. A respectable father and his daughter. Everything is all right.*

A tram rattled into the village and she thought for a moment about rushing across the road to catch it. But it was too public. Too slow. The thought of him erupting on the tram, where everyone might see.

She pulled him to the cabman's stand, where the one-horse hansom cabs were lined up.

'Where to, sir?' the driver called.

'Twelve Alcester Road,' she said. 'Go via Trafalgar Road.'

'Righto, miss.'

She pushed her father up into the cab and scrambled in beside him. With a snap of a whip, they were away up the hill. As they passed St. Mary's, she noticed the mourners hadn't come out yet and sighed with relief.

— 7 —

Once they were back at Uni, they bustled into a lecture theatre and stared blankly while Mr Fenwick talked through a Powerpoint about local history resources.

Rachel took notes but couldn't help glancing over at Danny, two rows below, scribbling away in his notebook. It was obvious from the way he worked so feverishly that he wasn't paying any attention to the lecture.

She craned to see over his shoulder. He was filling a page with images and words, some kind of mind map exercise. She could make out snatches of phrases written in bold strokes: *Amy Parker, Edwardian? 12 Alcester Road, Father? Funeral, "Is he the one?"* and the single word *TOUCHSTONE*.

A sketch of a girl in a black gown and a man in a top hat with a cane. The girl's face, again and again, trying to get the likeness just right. He was a decent artist.

His friends looked at him working hard and giggled, and when he became aware of them, he closed his notebook, sat back, and pretended to look bored, but she saw him open it again later and scribble some more things down.

When the lecture was over, he walked straight out, leaving everyone staring after him, wondering what was up.

She didn't see him the rest of the day as she worked in the library. Had he walked out and gone back to the churchyard to try it again without her? She cursed herself. She should have suggested that to him, not tonight. He would do it without her now.

She realized what she was thinking. It was ridiculous. But she'd seen it in his face. He believed it — and whatever it was that had happened to him, and the naked honesty and confusion in his manner had made her believe it too. A tiny part of her wanted to believe it, just to be able to share it with him.

After her final lecture, she drifted out. The sun was low in the sky as she waited for a bus. Only four o'clock and already night. A bus pulled up and she realized she might not have any money. She dug in her purse and pulled out a few coins. Not enough. Her face reddened.

She stepped out of the way, mumbling something under her breath, and let the passengers behind her get on. She stood there as it closed its doors and sailed off without her, swearing at herself under her breath. Then she saw the car behind the bus.

Jessica at the wheel. Stacy and Tyrone. Danny in the back, not talking. He saw her and looked back after her. She caught a flash of Jessica's laughing face as they sped off up the long road.

She started walking.

— 8 —

Home was thick with the smell of fried onions. Olive had cooked tea all afternoon. Crispy, dried out sausages in a gloopy gravy, mashed potatoes, fat slivers of fried onion, peas that had been boiled for about an hour.

Rachel attacked it, even though there was plenty of time to make the six o'clock rendezvous. They sat at the table but the telly was still on across the room.

'Well?' said Martyn.

She looked up at him and swallowed. 'Lots of things,' she said. 'Stuff.'

'Like?'

'Local history. We've got a seminar on you next week.'

Olive laughed.

'And you've joined the Stand-Up Comedy Society,' said Martyn.

'She gets that from you,' said Olive.

'Yeah, it's your fault,' said Rachel. He was still waiting for her to report on her day so she sighed and told him. 'We walked around St Mary's church yard and looked at the gravestones, then we went back to Uni and had a lecture on local history resources and I spent the afternoon in the library researching how Moseley used to be independent of Birmingham and why it took so long to join the big city.'

Martyn pointed his fork at her, with a bit of gravy-coated sausage on the end. 'Because Moseley's always been stuck up,' he said.

'That's where your great grandma was christened,' said Olive. 'My mum. When we lived round the corner. Down Anderton Park Road. Number 28. She was born there. So was I. And your dad. Beautiful big house.'

Rachel had heard this a million times. 'I know, I know,' she sighed. 'We used to be rich. How *did* you lose the family fortune, Dad?'

'I spent it on women and booze,' he smiled. 'The rest I wasted.' He laughed at his own joke.

'And now we have to live in poverty.' Rachel scowled.

'It'll make you more ambitious,' he said. 'Rich kids are bone idle and they get rubbish degrees. You'll thank me for growing up a pauper when you graduate with honours.'

He winked. She rolled her eyes.

As soon as tea was over, she washed up and ran to her room to change. She picked out a maxi skirt and the black velvet jacket she'd bought from the Goth shop in Oasis market; an outfit she used to wear when she was more self-conscious about her body and wanted to hide it. It seemed right tonight and would pass for Edwardian, if this whole thing wasn't a very elaborate joke. She sat on her bed and thought about that for twenty minutes. What if it was? What if she got there and they were all waiting for her in the churchyard, waiting to laugh and point? Stupid Rachel thought she was coming for some time travel! What a loser! Her stomach lurched. No, why would they do that? Danny's distress had been so genuine. She remembered the beads of sweat glistening on his temple. He wasn't that good an actor. No one was.

There was only one way to find out. She got up and walked down the stairs, calling out that she'd be back in an hour or two.

— 9 —

Amy Parker's ankle throbbed. When she had fallen in the churchyard, she'd thought she'd twisted it, but as she'd rushed her father onto the hansom cab, she'd felt nothing. Only now did it hurt.

She limped through to the kitchen and turned on the gas lamp. It hummed and cast a warm glow across the black range where Ida had left pans bubbling.

Perhaps the need to hide her father away had overcome everything else. If the need were great enough, the body would overcome any disability.

She grabbed a tea towel and opened the oven door. A blast of delicious heat hit her face. Pork belly shuddering in an enamel pot.

It smelled ready, but father was still asleep.

She closed the oven door and limped back to the parlour. It was best to let him sleep. It was safer. She would ignore her hunger all night if he might stay asleep. The body would overcome.

But her belly grumbled and she swooned with desire, slumping into the armchair by the meagre fire, holding a cushion to her belly.

Potatoes, pork belly and peas.

It wasn't much, but one had to be grateful. It was certainly more than Ida would get at home in Highgate. It seemed unfair, somehow, that Ida would prepare a meal for them every afternoon and leave it for them, before going home to eat dripping on bread.

There was a time when Ida would have eaten her own dinner in the scullery, and retired to her own room in the loft. But the Parkers no longer employed a domestic. It was Amy's job to serve dinner, eaten with her father in cold silence in the dining room, the dirty plates left in the sink for Ida to wash in the morning.

Her mother's face gazed down on her, frozen in monochrome.

When she'd died, the socialising had stopped. There were no more dinner parties where the Parker family could entertain their friends with several courses of the finest food. There were no more French dishes. There were no more friends.

The food had become simpler, more functional. Amy served it at the table every night and ate in silence, her father staring at the window to the front garden and the road outside where the trams passed, as if he might see his wife return and apologise for being late.

Pork belly and potatoes. It wasn't quite the level of a labourer, but how long before it was?

Gazing into the embers, she wondered at the strange boy again. What sort of name was *Danny*. Was it what the working classes called Daniel? He hadn't seemed so common. He had more of an aristocratic air. Perhaps that was it. He was posher than she was. She was stuck in the middle.

Was he a magician? A parlour trickster, like granny Parker? The whispers about the séances she held in the front parlour. Adult talk, quickly hushed over. Father would never talk about it. Her mother had gossiped with friends about it. Amy had overheard them talking over tea, thinking she didn't understand.

Richard's mother was a psychic. They came to this house from far and wide to talk to the dead. No wonder she ended up in the *whisper, whisper, whisper.*

Was it the fate of the family to fall into madness?

Grandma Parker, and poor uncle Herbert, who'd taken to drink and was frequently seen skulking in the churchyard with only a bottle for company. Thank God he hadn't been there today. He'd known Mr Rieper and would have paid his respects at the funeral, but evidently had enough shame not to show his face.

And father? He too was mad.

The family was sinking. Like the Titanic. Somewhere, long ago, an iceberg had struck, and every member of the family was drowning in the dark waters.

They were doomed.

'Amy!'

Her heart thumped in her throat and she jumped up, the cushion falling into the hearth.

He came clumping down the hall, his footsteps booming on the floorboards.

Fee fie fo fum.

The door flew back and she stood frozen in his glare, stammering, 'Father, you're awake. Dinner's ready. I've set the dining table. I'll bring it through to you.'

'Was he the one?'

The heart that thumped in her throat sank to the pit of her stomach.

'I don't know what that means, father.'

'You brought him to us. You called him.'

'No, father, no. I didn't.'

'You called the devil. Here. To our home.'

'I didn't do anything, father. He was just a boy passing by.'

He scrambled back to the hall and snatched up the stick.

'You made me do this, damn you, Amy.'

'No, father, please.'

He pointed to the dining room. There was no escaping this. She had thought he might sleep and forget but she had known it would come to this.

Head bowed, she skulked past him, down the hall to the front room. The dining table laid out for dinner. The table where Grandma Parker had summoned the dead.

Her father followed close behind, panting, a harsh gob of phlegm catching in his chest. He was sinking fast. Would he be alive this time next year?

'I don't know who that boy is, father, I swear it's true.'

'Do not lie to your God, or your father.'

She put her hands on the table and bowed down till her forehead met the cold mahogany.

'Forgive me for what I'm about to do,' he said.

She was about to say she forgave him and that he didn't need to do it, but realized he wasn't talking to her at all.

The stick hissed.

Thwack.

She yelped. It came out of her, unbidden, like a dog's bark.

Another hiss and

Thwack.

He groaned with the effort, a sob catching in his throat.

Thwack.

Hot tears sprang to her eyes. No matter how much you said you wouldn't cry, how much you said you would bear it in silence, you couldn't stop that.

Thwack.

We are losing our way. The ship is sinking. Water is pouring in.

Thwack.

Such certainty they had, those poor people. Even at the end, when the ship was low in the icy water, they still believed it was unsinkable.

Thwack.

The icy waters were rising through the lower decks. Soon the ship would split asunder and the end would come swiftly. What was it they had said? It was there in the dark water, still so magnificent, and then in a matter of minutes it slid under and was gone.

'There,' her father said. 'You make it so hard for me, who has to fight the evil that assails us.'

She pushed herself up from the table, the imprint of her hot cheek fading in the mahogany, afraid to look at him, afraid she might wet herself.

'I'm sorry, father.'

'I know, yet still you turn to sin. Time and time again. How am I to save you, Amy?'

'I don't know, father. But I'm glad you try.'

'Now go to your room. No food for you tonight.'

She walked to the foot of the stairs, faint with pain and hunger, each step burning agony. Clutching the banister, she inched up the steps, one at a time, a mountain to climb, praying that she might not faint before she reached her bed.

As she reached the top of the first flight and heard the chink of cutlery, she wondered what lifeboat might possibly save her.

— 10 —

Danny walked north up Alcester Road, taking a detour so he could look at the house where Amy Parker said she lived, a hundred years ago.

He wished he'd arranged to meet Rachel earlier. They could have sacked off Uni for the afternoon and gone straight back to the... *touchstone,* he'd decided to call it. It would be pitch black in the graveyard when they...

He stopped himself even thinking it. The whole thing was ridiculous. Which was probably why he was late and dawdling, reluctant to set out, and had circled round the opposite direction. It must have been the hangover this morning. He'd imagined it all, suffered an elaborate hallucination. It could all be explained scientifically. He'd probably caught something that had messed with his mind. He should go to the doctor. He'd been burning the candle at both ends since starting Uni. Perhaps that was it.

Except he knew that wasn't it. He'd felt it and seen it, and touched it and smelled it. He could still almost taste it. It had been all too real. Hyperreal.

He wondered why he'd even agreed to involve Rachel. It was nothing to do with her. It wasn't their secret, it was his. Only, he'd told her about it, and somehow he felt that she *was* involved. She was a part of it. He just didn't know why.

He stopped and looked across the road at the reason for his detour.

Number 12.

Right about now, Amy Parker was there, a hundred years ago. Somehow, those two times were happening at the same time, and he had found a bridge between the two.

A large terraced house, probably split into student rooms now. A small garden at the front. It looked unspectacular, and a little shabby now, but you could imagine that once it would have been impressive. A family of means would have lived here. Further up the road, there was a row of houses with uniform railings that had been restored to their former glory. He could easily imagine it was just the kind of place where gentlemen in top hats would return after a day at the bank.

To the north was the Moseley Dance Centre and the old tram depot, which was now a skate park, its crumbling façade covered in graffiti.

Amy Parker was there now… a hundred years ago.

He rushed on up the hill back to Moseley village, hoping he'd be able to see for himself soon.

— 11 —

Rachel walked down St Mary's Row and turned into the churchyard under the lychgate. No winos there tonight huddled under the wooden awning as they were most evenings. She walked up the winding path, glancing back to see if anyone had noticed her entering the churchyard alone at night. She stepped carefully over the buckled paving where they'd all stood this morning listening to Mr Fenwick and wondered if he did that thing every year with each new class, relishing the shock as they realized they were standing on old gravestones.

Arabella Palmer, who departed this life August 16th 1876.

Aged 8 years or 38 years. A girl just like her who had lived and died right here. She wondered what kind of life she'd lived, what she'd seen, and how different it had been from Rachel's life.

Then she wondered if she could go back and find out.

Of course, she thought. *This* was the person they should research for their project. It didn't matter that the grave was now a paving slab; it was still a name on a gravestone in that churchyard.

She walked round the church and took the path down to the gate. Floodlights that lit up the church meant that it wasn't so dark. No one seemed to be hanging around in there.

She reached the gravestone where they'd sat this morning. No Danny. She looked all around, hands thrust in her coat pockets, trying to act nonchalant. What if he'd already... gone through? Should she try it herself? If she reached out and touched it where he'd touched it, would they all leap out from behind trees and bushes and laugh at her? Stacy, Jessica, Tyrone and Danny.

She looked around again, trying to peer through the murk. She stopped breathing and listened for any slight sound of shuffling or stifled giggles. There was nothing but the drone of traffic and the faint hubbub of talk from the village: people gathering for the bars.

She took her hands from her pockets and edged closer to the gravestone, casting one more furtive glance around the graveyard. She reached out, her fingers groping for the spot where he'd touched it this morning, where she'd almost touched it herself before Mr Fenwick had interrupted.

Her fingertips stroked the rough stone surface, cold to the touch.

A candle burned her finger, an angel breathed in her ear, the light changed, her ears rang and she was staring into a bearded face, choking on a hot blast of whiskey breath. Her hand was on the stone and the man's thighs were either side of it. She yelped.

He snarled, dropped his bottle, jumped up and snatched her hair. She screamed, tried to twist away, head burning.

'Hey! What's going on!' he spluttered.

She reeled backwards, crying out, eyes clenching shut as he raised his dirty fist to hit her.

— 12 —

The man shouted again and there was a slapping sound, just once. He grabbed her arm and yanked her away.

She opened her eyes to find it was Danny pulling her towards the gate. She looked back to see the drunk scrambling in the soft grass for his peaked cap.

'Come on!' said Danny.

He pushed through the wrought-iron gate and closed it behind them. They watched the drunk climb back to his feet and dust himself down. He shouted something and shook his fist but he was more interested in finding his bottle. Once he'd found it and picked it up, he shuffled off. She breathed again. They were safe.

'He scared me to death. I came through and had my hand between his legs.'

'It's okay,' said Danny. 'We're safe. I think.'

They turned and looked down the alley and gaped in wonder. It wasn't the same alley they'd walked down this morning. In the darkness, she could make out a wide triangle of waste ground, not an alley. Further down was a slit of light. A man walked past in a bowler hat. The space down there was screened off by a giant billboard.

'Come on,' he said.

They pinheaded towards the door of dim light. She held

her hand out in front of her, wishing she'd brought a torch.

'Wait.' She took out her phone and pressed the torchlight app. Blue light lit the way. To the side were rows of giant barrels. The Bull's Head pub was the building to the left, she realized.

'There's no Barclays bank,' she said.

The building with its Ionic columns that had looked over the village green all her life wasn't there, which was why it wasn't really an alley.

Danny still had hold of her hand and seemed to realize for the first time. He mumbled something, looked down at the floor and let go of her.

She followed him towards the strip of light at the end, and peered out, gasping aloud at what they saw.

The village green lit by gaslamps – a busy crossroads hub of horse-drawn coaches, electric trams and promenading Edwardians. It was like turning a corner and walking into a film set. They stood there frozen, mouths agape in wonder.

'Oh my God,' she managed to say.

'It's true,' he said.

'This is really…' She floundered for the word, but nothing came. There was no word for it.

'Yeah,' he said.

'When are we?'

'I don't know.'

On the village green were a couple of wooden huts. The larger one stood roughly where the bus stop was, a row of horses and carriages waited. A cabman's shelter. The smaller hut stood in the middle of the green and seemed to be a newsstand, manned by a shabby old man in a peaked cap, a muffler wrapped round his face.

An electric tram deposited a stream of bowler-hatted gentlemen and women in long dresses and large hats.

'There,' said Danny. 'Come on.'

He stepped out of cover and walked across the sliproad to

the green. Rachel watched him go, cringing inside, feeling that if they stepped foot in this world something awful would happen. If they stood and stared from the safety of the alley's mouth, maybe no one would see them.

She didn't want to be alone so she scurried after him to the newsstand, where several people who'd got off the tram were buying the evening edition.

Danny grabbed a newspaper from the stand and looked at the front page. It was called *The Birmingham Gazette & Express*.

'Hey! That's threepence.'

'I'm just looking,' said Danny.

'I'll give you *just looking*, you cheeky…'

The shabby old newsstand man stopped and stared at Danny.

'Hang on,' he said.

'Danny,' said Rachel, pulling on his arm.

'Sorry,' said Danny, dropping the newspaper.

'Here, wait!' the newsstand man cried.

Rachel pulled Danny away, turning to notice the billboard that stood in place of Barclays Bank was a giant advertisement for Oxo. They crossed the narrow slip road and stopped at the alley's dark mouth.

'It's today,' he hissed.

'What?'

She frog-marched him back into the darkness. Glancing back, she saw the newsstand man staring after them. There was something about his look that wasn't right.

'It's today's date,' said Danny.

'Today? That doesn't make sense.'

'It's the 22nd of November. But in 1912.'

He pulled her up the dark alley, heading for the gate to the churchyard.

'Why are we going back?' she asked.

He suddenly seemed terrified. The whole thing had

spooked him and he wanted to run back to the present, to safety. But with a coldness she only noted later, he said, 'We need clothes and we need money.'

— 13 —

Danny peeked through the church gate. The drunk was still there, sitting at another stone, talking to himself.

'Quick.'

He pulled the gate open. The hinges whined. Too loud. They ran for it and reached the stone. Rachel touched it first.

Danny looked at the drunk, who staggered to his feet and growled something incoherent. Rachel wasn't there anymore. Danny grinned as the drunk lunged for him.

'See ya. Wouldn't wanna be ya.'

He touched the stone and there was a flash of confusion, like he'd been punched and hadn't seen it coming. He found himself staring at the same spot. The drunk had disappeared. The buzz of traffic was in his ears again.

'Are you all right?' said Rachel.

'I think we're back.'

The floodlights in the graveyard. It was much brighter.

'I can hear the traffic,' she said. 'I feel sick.'

'We've just travelled a hundred years in a split second.'

'1912!' Rachel screamed.

They laughed hysterically. This was crazy.

'1912!'

They hugged each other and danced around, then broke away and collected themselves.

'I don't believe this,' she squealed. 'It's actually true!'

'It can't be,' he said. 'But we saw it.'

She ran over to another gravestone and stroked her hands along it.

'What are you doing?'

'Maybe they all work,' she said. 'Maybe this one takes you to a different year.'

'Don't be ridiculous,' he said.

But why wouldn't others do it? He tried one himself, running his fingers across the stone. They skipped from stone to stone, trying every one, but nothing happened.

She returned breathless to theirs. 'So it's just this one. And we're the only people who know about it.'

'Maybe.'

'It's our secret, right? No one else?'

He thought about it. What was it about Rachel being so desperate to keep it between the two of them? As if he'd want to tell idiots like Stacy, Jessica and Tyrone.

'Okay,' he said. 'Just us.'

She smiled and he realized he didn't actually like his 'friends' any more than she did. He didn't trust them at all. He didn't really trust anyone. He only regretted he'd discovered this in the company of Rachel. If not, he'd have it all to himself now.

'We need to research this,' he said. 'Find out what 1912 is all about. We can get clothes and old money in the morning. There's that junk shop up the road and the fancy dress hire place opposite.'

'We can't do it in the morning,' she said. 'Field trip to the library.'

'Okay, straight after, then.'

They walked up the path and he looked back, thinking how strange it was that the drunk wasn't still there in the churchyard behind them — he was a hundred years ago.

— 14 —

Rachel ran home and rushed to her room, where she paced around, burning with excitement. She'd seen it: her own neighbourhood, exactly as it was a century ago. She threw herself on her bed and thought of all the things she could do.

Would it always be exactly 100 years ago on the other side? If she went through again tomorrow, would the drunk still be there, just as he was when she'd left him, or maybe even earlier? Could she meet herself back there? What if she went back and it were 1940? Or 1936? Or 1966? Or the eighties?

Maybe she could go back and see her mum.

The thought of it brought tears to her eyes. She fantasized about going back to see her before she'd died, when Rachel was too young to remember anything but a Christmas morning blur; an impression of tinsel, glittering presents under a tree, the scent of pine, a woman in a beige sweater, smiling. It was like a half-developed Polaroid in her mind, maddeningly out of focus; like a familiar melody she couldn't quite place, always out of reach.

She went downstairs to the dining table to write up her coursework, but she couldn't concentrate on it. Martyn and Olive were watching TV across the room. She had an idea suddenly and went to one of the sideboard cupboards and rummaged around.

'What you looking for, Rache?' said Martyn.

'The old photos.'

'They're in the Black Magic box,' said Olive.

'I know, but I can't see it.'

Olive was already at her side, looking for something to do. You could never do anything without her appearing at your side to help you. 'They're on the other side, love.'

She looked in the other cupboard and pulled it out: an old Black Magic chocolate box from the 1960s. She placed it reverently on the dining table and took off the lid. It was crammed full of old snapshots, faded photos of distant relatives, all jumbled up in no particular order.

'We should really get a photo album for these,' said Olive.

She'd been saying that Rachel's entire life and it had never happened. Rachel quietly noted the idea of buying some albums and those little mounting stickers for Nan's birthday. It would be a nice project for her.

She emptied the photos out, scattering them all over the table.

'That's the old house,' said Olive, picking up a creased black and white snap. It showed Olive as a girl posing with her parents outside the old house. 'That was during the war, that was.'

Rachel flipped the photo over and read the pencilled inscription on the back.

'1940.' She picked up another. 'Who's this, Nan?'

A woman standing in the same spot on a different day, a baby in her arms. The baby was mostly a white over-exposed blur and you could only tell it was a baby by the way she was carrying it. The woman was plump and frowning.

'That's my grandma. Grandma Lewis.'

Rachel looked at the back. '*Mary Lewis, with baby Winnie. 1913.* Winnie was your mum?'

'Yes.'

'And the family used to own that big house?'
'Oh yes, we were very posh.'

Rachel gazed at the photo of Mary Lewis, matching her great-great-grandmother's frown.

She went through the photos with Olive, listening to the stories about her relatives who'd lived in Moseley the last 100 years or more, and chose a small stack of a dozen or more to take with her.

She knew exactly what she was going to do back in 1912 now.

— 15 —

Joe Rees cut the mastheads off the newspapers that hadn't been sold and added them to the pile that would be returned at the end of the week. He stacked the orphaned newspapers, tied them into a bundle and left them on the floor of the hut. Normally he would take them home, but tonight he needed a strong one.

He pulled the shutter in and hooked the clasp, stepped out of the cabin and locked it. A tram pulled in, sparks raining off the power line, and unloaded a phalanx of commuters from the city. Might have sold the last of the papers there. One or two gentlemen walked straight into the Bulls Head and the Fighting Cocks.

A ghost.

He had walked right up and picked up a paper in daylight as broad as Broad Street. A ghost. As real as that woman walking home with her basket tucked under her arm.

Except, if it was his ghost, he was younger, much younger than when Joe had last seen him.

I'm just looking.

It had even sounded like him.

Joe marched across the green, looked left, let a hansom clatter past heading up St. Mary's, crossed and walked straight into the saloon of the Bull's Head.

Warm fog of tobacco smoke, sawdust and beer. Behind the bar a boy done up in a stiff collar and waistcoat, so young looking he wouldn't get served.

Dyke Wilkinson puffed on a pipe, in his billycock hat and whiskers, forever looking like he was setting off out of the door.

'Evening, sir,' said the boy. 'What can I get you?'

Joe bumped the bar. 'A pint of Burton's dinner ale, young man,' he said. They had a bloody familiar way of addressing their elders and betters, these lads.

The boy poured his pint and Joe handed over threepence, collected his drink and edged to the rear of the bar.

If you died and became a ghost, did you come back as your younger self? Was there a rule for that?

He knocked back the pint and put a good half of it down. Needed it. Shock.

There was no such thing as ghosts. Only women believed that kind of nonsense. There was science and facts. Like in a broadsheet. Facts in plain old black and white. That was what the newspapers were.

But the news wasn't about facts anymore. No one knew that more than a newsvendor. You had the broadsheets with their acres of print, and you could rely on that for Objective Truth. But there were other kinds of paper, like The Illustrated Police News. The worst newspaper in England, they called it. He'd always sold that paper, right from the start. It sold well in Birmingham. If there was one thing people liked more than a lurid crime story, it was a lurid crime story with pictures. Blood and murder. Husbands turning violent, fathers killing their children. Madness, blood, evil. It had built Joe Rees's business empire – a shed that sat on Moseley village green. It had bought this pint.

That and being a Harvey Duff.

He took out the old brooch he had pinned inside his jacket lapel, and turned it over in the gaslight. An old penny that someone had turned into a brooch, with an engraving of a zephyr blowing wind from furious cheeks and the letters D and M in ornate filigree.

A ghost.

Someone barging towards him across the bar. He looked up expecting to see Daniel Pearce again, but it was only Herbert Parker staggering in.

He caught Joe's eye and grinned. 'Evening, Joe.'

'Evening, Herbert. How are you?'

'Dry.'

After a pint. A sponger, a waster. Not like that brother of his, a respectable chartered accountant in the city and one of them funny handshaking masons. Herbie was the runt of the family – the bad one who was on the skids. Every family has one, I guess, thought Joe. And if you don't know who it is in your family, then it's probably you.

Dyke Wilkinson stepped forward, pointing his pipe. 'Now don't you disturb my clientele, Herbert. Out with you.'

'He's all right,' said Joe. 'I owe him one.'

Herbert belched and tottered round in a circle and tipped his hat, glassy eyed. 'A mild, please.'

Dyke Wilkinson poured the beer and slid it across the bar. 'Just the one, mind,' he said. 'You look like you've had a skinful already.'

What was it with landlords? Their trade was getting good men jiggered, so why did they always object when a customer looked as drunk as a boiled owl? You'd think they'd be happy.

'He's all right, Dyke. I'll make sure he's out of here after this.'

'He's a gentleman, he is,' Herbert slurred. 'A true gentleman.'

Dyke came over and leaned close. 'Are you all right, though, Joe? You look as if you've seen a ghost.'

Joe put on a smile. 'All is well. To tell you the truth, I could do with a bit of company tonight.'

Anyone. Even Half-Shot Herbert.

'I seen a ghost too,' said Herbert.

Dyke walked off to serve another customer and Herbert gulped down half his pint.

'Standing in front of me like you're in front of me now. A bloody ghost. Disappeared. Pff! Like that.'

'That must have been a terrible shock for you, Herbert.'

Herbert waved his hand dismissively. As drunk as he was, he knew when someone was codding him on, and didn't care if it was someone who had just paid for his pint.

'The problem with this place is, with Moseley is, everyone thinks their money's from a different mint.'

'Yes, Herbert.'

'Take my brother, for instance. Turfed me out of house and home. My own brother.'

Joe supped at his ale and found himself far away, only half listening to Herbert's rant about his brother.

It couldn't have been him. It was impossible. And it couldn't have been a ghost. That was impossible too. So if it looked exactly like him, but younger, it could only mean it was Daniel Pearce's *son*. It must be.

And the son might know where the father was.

'Thinks he's so high and mighty, looking down his long nose at me. I could tell a few things about what he gets up to. It'd knock the smile right off the reverend's face.'

You couldn't go to the police with tales about ghosts and men who aged backwards. You needed a good solid fact. And Daniel Pearce's son walking through Moseley village was a good solid fact. Even though a son was kind of like a ghost.

He totted up quick arithmetic on his fingers.

1888. Ninety-eight is ten and oh-eight twenty plus four is twenty-four. It was twenty-four years ago. Dear God, how the time flies.

If this were Daniel Pearce's son, he would have to have had the boy after he'd disappeared from Birmingham. There was no way the lad who'd walked right up to Joe and tried to steal a paper was any older than twenty.

And that meant Daniel Pearce might still be alive.

These were the kind of facts that would definitely interest Inspector Beadle, who hadn't paid Joe Rees nearly so much money for information as he ought to have lately.

Joe downed his pint, wiped the froth from his moustache, and tipped his hat to the landlord. He was out the door before poor, addled Herbert knew he was gone, striding across the green to the tram stop on the other side.

He could reacquaint himself with Inspector Beadle after a good night's sleep. If he felt as sure about it in the light of day, he'd go straight to the police station and tell him that an old ghost had returned, like a murderer to the scene of the crime.

— 16 —

Rachel sat on the steps in Chamberlain Square, her back to the early morning rush of office workers, sketching out a family tree in her notebook. She liked to sit in the south-west corner next to the sculpture of Thomas Attwood that lounged across the steps, hidden away, a secret; his sheets of bronze paper flying across the steps behind him. It had always made her feel close to history, as if she were sitting with this man from the past, he writing on his sheet of paper with his quill; she writing in her notebook. As if they could co-exist, side by side, through a space of 150 years.

It was more than an idle fantasy now. It was real. She really could do that. Perhaps she could go back to 1832 and see him become the first MP for Birmingham. The possibilities had been buzzing inside her all night and she couldn't think of anything else.

The council house clock tolled ten so she put her notebook and stack of family photos in her bag and twisted to her feet.

'Bye, Thomas.'

She turned to see the cluster of students outside the brutalist concrete block of the Central Library and Mr Fenwick arriving to greet them. She climbed the steps and joined the group, nodding to Danny.

Mr Fenwick had just finished speaking when she got there. He walked into the 1960s concrete and glass building and they followed him in, through the foyer and up the series of escalators, snaking up to the sixth floor and the Local Studies section. It felt strange to be coming here for study, when she'd come here so many times for pleasure, just to read and look up things for her own amusement, ever since she'd been about twelve.

Mr Fenwick took them round the department and pointed out the various resources he'd covered in his lecture yesterday and they split off into their project pairs and spread out to claim different desks in the acres of book-lined space.

As soon as Nick had pointed out the computers that stored the local newspaper facsimiles, Danny had sat straight down and looked one up. When the front page splashed across the screen, he grinned like he'd invented it himself. It was the *Birmingham Gazette & Express* they'd been looking at last night. She felt a thrill go through her. Here it was on a computer screen and she'd seen it only last night, the real thing, freshly printed.

'It's just mad, isn't it,' she said.

'So, I've been thinking,' he said. 'We don't do this Rees or Read or whoever it is. We do her instead.'

'Who?'

'Amy Parker. The girl I met when I went through the touchstone the first time.'

'You know that's not what the word touchstone means, right?'

'It's what I'm calling it,' he said, opening his notebook at the page of notes and sketches he'd made in the lecture. Seeing it close up, Rachel could tell he was good. Better than she'd thought.

She looked at her own notebook with her scribbled inscription of the gravestone details. It seemed feeble and tiny and dwarfed by his effort. His notebook was even twice the size of hers, a great canvas for inspirational broad-brush strokes, hers, a secret depository of spidery meanderings no one could read.

'You're a really good artist,' she said. 'Why aren't you at art school?'

'My mum thinks training to be an artist is a waste of a degree. I'd be poor the rest of my life.'

'And she thought a History degree would really be a ticket to wealth?'

'It's a compromise.'

'This Amy Parker isn't one of the names in the churchyard,' Rachel said, but she knew as she said it that it would make no difference.

'So what? Just tell Nick we're doing this instead. He'll let us. He likes you.'

He got up and headed for the information desk.

'No he doesn't,' she said. But Danny had already gone.

The woman behind the information desk was young, but her thick black glasses and red hair pinned up in a bun made it look as if she acting the archetypal librarian. Danny looked at her name badge and turned on the charm.

'Excuse me… Kath,' he said. 'Can you help me?'

'I'll try my best,' she said.

Rachel wanted to vomit. He was practically undressing her with his eyes and she was encouraging him.

'If I wanted to find out all about a person from a hundred years ago,' he said. 'Where would I look here?'

'Take your pick,' she said, smiling a little too warmly for a librarian. 'We've got a whole floor of resources. How much do you know already?'

'Well, we've got a name, an address, and the year. She's about my age in 1912, I think.'

'Well, you could start with the births and deaths fiches. Once you know the birth date, you can buy a birth certificate from the Register Office round the corner. Same with a death certificate. Then you can take it from there.'

'Thank you, Kath. That's very helpful.'

Kath smiled and went to fetch the box of fiches for him.

He turned to Rachel. 'I'll look up Amy, you look up her father. It's Parker, 12 Alcester Road.'

Rachel stared at him with disgust.

'What?' he said.

'Old enough to be your mum.'

She walked off to get a microfiche reader. Mr Fenwick was there leaning over Jessica and Stacy, trying to show them how to use it, which seemed to be difficult, largely because they couldn't work out why they couldn't touch the screen to operate it.

'No, look, you've put it in the wrong way. Flip it over. You see?'

'And we have to look through all that lot?' said Stacy.

'Won't take you long. You've already got year to work from.'

Rachel coughed and he turned to her. 'Er, Nick?'

'Rachel.'

'If we've got an address, right, and a year, is there any way of finding out who was living there then?'

He looked at her curiously but didn't ask why. 'I'll show you.'

As she followed him to the other side of the Local Studies section, she heard Jessica put on a Brummie accent.

'Nick? If we've got an address, roit, and a year, roit…'

'Did you see her *shoes*?' said Stacy.

'My god, she must have got them at the Rag Market.'

Nick strolled into a row of stacks lined with directories and Rachel followed, her face burning with anger.

'Normally, you'd look in the Census, but if you know the address, and it's within the last hundred years, you've got these little beauties. Kelly's Directories.'

He stroked his fingers along the rows of red and black

books. Rachel picked out the Directory for 1912 and leafed through it.

'Go to the *Streets* section and you can find out the head of the household.'

'This is it,' she said. 'Twelve, Alcester Road. Mr Richard Parker.'

'Why are you starting from an address anyway?'

She looked up into his eyes. 'Er, we're not doing the name from the grave. We're doing a girl called Amy Parker. We know she lived there in 1912.'

'You're supposed to do someone buried in St Mary's.'

'We'll do a great project, I promise.'

He looked over his shoulder and leaned in closer. 'Do not. Tell. The others.'

He tapped his nose and she walked back to find Danny. He was staring at the white-on-black text on the enormous microfiche reader screen.

'The father's called Richard Parker,' she said. 'Have you found Amy?'

He had that look again. Almost like when she'd come back to find him sitting on the gravestone.

'Yeah,' he said.

He pointed at the screen. She leaned over him to look.

'She dies in three days' time.'

— 17 —

Inspector Beadle scanned the overnight arrest sheets from the various police stations under his command. Balsall Heath had been busy, as usual, Kings Norton less so. Here at Moseley Police Station on Woodbridge Road, there had been two domestics and a drunk starting a fight in the Bull's Head. He checked the desk calendar and for the fifth time that week, he noted the full moon was on Saturday. Always when the incidents increased.

He took the arrest sheet out and examined the mugshot clipped to the charge sheet. Herbert's familiar scowl.

If only he'd taken Macpherson's suggestion on board years ago: to put Herbert Parker in a paddy wagon, take him for a long ride, and throw him out in Wolverhampton or Smethwick. Let him be someone else's problem for a month or so, till he found his way back.

Leafing through the Balsall Heath reports, he found that most of it concerned a variety 'theatre' that was a brothel in all but name. The kind of place where young girls entertained on the stage and the same young girls entertained old men from the audience backstage. No one paid for this entertainment, but the Champagne, which was little more than cheap carbonated wine, was expensive, and the gentlemen were encouraged to buy a great quantity of it.

Once or twice a week, the 'theatre' would erupt, usually when one of the lower orders resented the conspicuous wealth of a toff, or a Peaky decided to relieve a gent of his pocket watch and wallet. Twenty-four years ago, you would have as likely seen an ostrich walking through Moseley village as a Peaky Blinder, but now they were virtually camped on the Moseley and Balsall Heath border. It was an invisible border, nothing more than Brighton Road, but it existed in the minds of the populace. The Peakies hadn't yet crossed it. They didn't need to. The toffs and shabby genteel of Moseley came to them. The brothels of Balsall Heath and Highgate were their watering hole.

Desk Sergeant Frank Donaghy clumped through, did his little cough, and rapped the door before walking in. 'Sir, there's someone here wants to see you. Asked specifically for you. Won't say what it is.'

'Who is it?'

'Fellah by the name of Joseph Rees. I can tell him to fill out a statement, if you want?'

Beadle pulled off his spectacles and sat back, humming to himself.

'Sir?'

'Show him through.'

'What? In here, sir? Your office?'

Beadle sighed. 'Donaghy. This was all rather before your time.'

Donaghy stepped further inside and closed the door behind him, sensing that his Inspector was taking him into his confidence. A rare event.

'Joe Rees is an ex-informant.'

'Ah, I see.'

'He keeps the news vendor's hut on Moseley village green, and has done since he was a boy. Built it up himself. He's served us well over many years, although I haven't had need of his services for quite a while.'

'So he might have something new?'

'Possibly. Or he might want money for old rope.'

'I'll show him through.'

Donaghy clumped back to the reception desk.

Joe Rees had always been reliable, back in the day. He'd given solid information. Thirty years ago one wouldn't have thought it was needed in a quiet, respectable suburb like Moseley, but even back then Birmingham had washed right up and wet everyone's feet, bringing with it a tide of scum.

The brothels and fleshpots of Calthorpe Park had spread to Highgate at first, and then the contagion had enveloped Balsall Heath. These places, once independent villages, had defected to Birmingham ten years ago. Before Moseley had succumbed to become a suburb, the corruption had already been rife.

And he did not kid himself that respectable, middle-class Moseley had always been entirely innocent. Quiet it might have been, but behind those net curtains and Aspidistra plants standing guard at every window, there was just as much greed, vice, murder. They marched to St Mary's every Sunday in their best clothes, but it didn't stop them coveting their neighbour's gold and killing them for it.

From the perspective of a Detective Inspector, Moseley had never been quiet.

The door opened again and Donaghy showed Joe through. Beadle rose and shook his hand.

'Joe, old friend. How good to see you.'

'How funny,' said Joe. 'We work closer to each other than ever, and I see you less.'

He twisted his cloth cap in his red hands.

'Sergeant. Some tea for us.'

'There's some on the boil,' said Donaghy. He scooted out.

'Take a seat and warm yourself.'

'Oh, I'm fine. I've come straight from home this morning. I'm out in all weathers, so it doesn't bother me.'

Beadle took his seat and surveyed him. There was something about Joe Rees that looked used up. Like some fickle god had taken his life, screwed it up and tossed it in the waste paper basket without another thought. Beadle wondered if that fickle god might have been himself.

'You look well on it,' he said. 'I wish I was out on the street more myself. They have me behind a desk most days now, shuffling papers.'

'Not like the old days, eh?' Joe laughed, a gleam in his eye. 'Running down Peakies and sloggers. It was like the Wild West at one point even.'

A shadow passed over Beadle's heart. 'Yes, quite. It's a lot more serene now.'

'Thanks to you, I suppose,' said Joe. 'The best policemen don't solve crimes, they make sure they never happen in the first place.'

Donaghy came back in with two cups of stewed brown tea and once he was gone and they had shared a few pleasantries, Beadle said, 'So, Joe. What brings you here?'

'Yesterday, I saw a... an old friend of ours.'

'Oh? And who was that?'

'Daniel Pearce.'

Joe chuckled, and Beadle was aware that he might have turned white. He took a sip of tea and grimaced. 'But that's impossible.'

'That's what I thought. But I saw him with these two eyes. Came right up to my stall and tried to steal a paper.'

'I'm not sure what you want me to... do,' said Beadle, aware that he was stalling, trying to think of what this meant.

'I was a police informer for years and this is an unsolved crime.'

'There was never any indication that it was him.'

'Perhaps so,' said Joe. 'But we all thought it. You thought it just as much as I did.'

Beadle sipped his tea again, shoved the cup to one side. It

was awful, and he suddenly felt quite queasy. 'Are you sure it was him?'

'I would normally stake my life on it. But the peculiar thing was, he looked younger than when he disappeared. If that's possible.'

Beadle sighed. 'Had you taken drink?'

'I'm not a drunk, sir. I've always drunk in moderation. I had a pint last night to steady me. It was the shock, you see. But that's a rare occurrence. A bartender has to ask me what I want when I walk in. They don't pour the usual before I reach the bar.'

'But still, Joe, this is nonsense.'

'I'm not like that Half-Cut Herbert, hugging the bar every night. He was there last night and all. Sloshed, as usual. Couldn't see a hole in a ladder. Compared to him I was as sober as a fish, and I know what I saw.'

There was something about Joe's vehemence. What Beadle had taken for the grizzled air of a hungover sot was something else. Genuine shock. He looked like a man who'd had Death brush past him.

'Here's the thing,' said Joe. 'Like I say. I *thought* it was him. Sounded like him, even. But it couldn't be. Unless he's taken to ageing backwards and has been getting younger instead of older. I wouldn't put that past him, mind. There was always something off about him. You know that.'

'So you saw someone who looked like him.'

'I saw his son. That's the only explanation. It's the only rational explanation.'

Beadle felt the room circling like a carousel. He shut his eyes and rubbed the bridge of his nose. He feared there was no rational explanation. He felt a merciless riptide pulling him back into a dark ocean.

'His son,' he said. 'Yes, that might make sense.'

'It's the only thing that does make sense,' said Joe.

Beadle opened his eyes and nodded, standing up, quickly

to business. Joe put his cup aside and stood, and Beadle walked him out to the reception. Seeing it empty, he sidled up to Sergeant Donaghy and in low tones told him Joe Rees was to have two shillings from petty cash. Donaghy pressed the coins into Joe's red palm and he pocketed them like a hungry bird taking a worm.

'Thank you, Joe. I'll follow this up. If you see anything else, give the usual signal. I'll instruct the constables on the Moseley beat to look out for it.'

Joe tipped his cap and chuckled. 'It's just like old days, sir. I do miss them.'

'I wonder if we're both a bit too old now for such adventure,' said Beadle.

'No one's ever too old.'

Joe left with a spring in his step and Beadle returned to his desk, scowling at the pile of reports from Balsall Heath. The truth was, he really was tired of adventure. Retirement was tantalisingly close and he was already settling into his slippers.

He stared into space for what might have been a half hour before he caught himself.

Opening his desk drawer, he pulled out a moleskin journal bound with a black ribbon, which he untied. He took out the eagle feather, its white still pristine as new snow, the tip as black as midnight. And a single scarlet spot painted in deep vermilion.

There were some things police reports could not explain away, and he'd seen a few. The redhead girl who'd left this feather behind was one. Daniel Pearce was another.

He'd seen other things, peculiar things, all noted down in this journal, kept from the official reports, but this was surely an old drunk talking nonsense.

He rushed to his bookcase and picked Kelly's Directory off the shelf. In the Court section, he found her.

Palmer, Arabella. Governess.

She was living in Kings Heath.

Beadle felt the familiar flutter in his guts. The feeling when a big case was near. So near you could taste it. That feeling when you were bearing down on a criminal and just about to collar him. He'd got his man, or woman, almost every time. He had failed only a few times. But those were the ones that haunted him.

And one of them might have swum right back into his net.

He reached for his hat and coat and rushed out of the station.

'I'll be a couple of hours,' he told Donaghy. 'I have to visit a suspect in Kings Heath.'

— 18 —

The Register Office building was a short walk away, behind Broad Street, and Rachel ran behind Danny as he marched, a man possessed now. She sat in the waiting lounge watching him pace up and down like an expectant father. Only this was about death, not new life.

'Won't it cause a rift in the space time continuum?' she said.

'You what?'

'That's what it does in films. You stop her from dying, then we come back to the present and find out the world's run by monkeys and we're their pets.'

'That's *Planet of the Apes,* stupid.'

'I'm just saying.'

'She looked healthy to me,' he said. 'It can't have been a disease or anything.'

'He recognized you.'

'What?'

'The old man selling the newspapers. He recognized you.'

Danny stopped pacing. 'How could he? I've never seen him before.'

'Well, he looked like he'd seen *you* before.'

'That's impossible.'

'So is travelling back in time by touching a stone.'

Danny looked around. Had anyone else in the waiting room heard that? There were only a couple of young mothers too busy with their new babies, and a podgy guy in a pork pie hat and a goatee beard, but he was staring into space, shell-shocked, red eyed. No one was listening to them.

'Keep it quiet, eh? We talked about it being a secret, between us, yeah?'

The desk clerk signalled him. He rushed over and took the two A4 envelopes. He sat down with her and handed her one. They both opened them and pulled out the green death certificates.

'What does yours say?' he said.

She checked Richard Parker's name and the panel where it listed the cause of death. 'General Paralysis.'

'What's General Paralysis?'

'I don't know,' she said. 'But whatever it is, he gets it in the City Asylum."

'Struth.'

'What does Amy's say?"

'Oh God.'

'What?' she said. 'What does Amy's say?'

He handed her the certificate. She stared at the single word in the column.

Murder.

— 19 —

Inspector Beadle took the electric tram through Moseley and on to Kings Heath. He had a personal coachman on hand, and there had been talk of providing him with a motor car, but he often preferred to walk the streets or take public transport. With a short jaunt like this, the electric tram presented a swift option that was convenient. Sitting side-by-side with real people kept him close to the community he policed. And for a few years now, he had felt more and more remote.

There was something exciting about the electric tram, anyway. The way it hummed, whirred and rattled along, swaying at corners and bends in the road, the rod sometimes sparking above. To be transported this way felt so modern.

He might have been old and ready for retirement, but he had no wish to cling to the old ways.

The tram conductor saluted as Beadle stepped off on Kings Heath High Street, busy with shoppers. He turned into Poplar Road at Lashford's butchers on the corner, still there after all these years. On Woodville Road, he found he was reciting the names of the villas in decorative plaster relief above each front door. He wondered what their connection might be, other than merely alphabetical.

Xanthus, Whitby, Verona, Ulster, Turin.

Weren't they all seaports around the world?

Savona, Ramsey, Quetta, Pendleton.

No, some of those were inland. Sites of military victories, perhaps, or great cities?

Olivencia, Newbiggen, Malmedy, Langholm.

All place names, certainly. Though was there any place in the world with the name Olivencia?

Kandapur, Jedburg, Illminster…

They had served as a sequence of identifiers before the street was numbered, of course, but was there a theme? There seemed no logic to it. Could it be a random sequence of names or was there a hidden meaning, a code that might be cracked?

He was a detective and saw a mystery to be solved in everything, but perhaps some patterns in the universe were simply random and were not puzzles to be solved. As he approached retirement, it was a disquieting thought.

He came to Arabella Palmer's house a little further on, an imposing terrace with a square of garden dominated by a hawthorn bush. He rattled the brass doorknocker and waited.

The woman who answered the door looked surprised, and he thought he had the wrong house.

'Miss Palmer?'

Then he saw it in her eyes. Recognition, followed by the involuntary inward wretch of a bad memory.

'Yes?' she said.

'Inspector Beadle.' He dug in his pocket for his credentials.

'I know,' she said. 'I remember.'

'Don't be alarmed,' he said. 'This is merely a courtesy call. If it's not inconvenient for you?'

She bit her lip and glanced back over her shoulder. The percussion of activity from inside. 'It's fine,' she said, 'Do come in.'

He followed her through the Menton-tiled hallway to the

rear parlour where five women sat around a dining table, a silver tea service in the centre.

'This is Inspector Beadle,' Arabella said.

The women around the table stiffened. One of them shot up from her chair and shouted, 'We're doing nothing wrong! You can't arrest us for talking!'

Beadle stared open-mouthed for a moment till he noticed the suffragist pamphlets on the table.

'Bertha, it's fine,' said Arabella. 'I'm sure Inspector Beadle hasn't come to discuss politics. At least I don't think he has.'

She turned to him with accusing eyes. They all glared, ready for a fight. He took his bowler off.

'Indeed, ladies, forgive the intrusion. I have come to discuss a private matter with Miss Palmer.'

The woman called Bertha looked to Arabella, whose cheeks had flushed crimson.

'Perhaps we can talk in the front parlour. Forgive me, ladies. Bertha, could you bring the inspector a cup of tea?'

Bertha nodded but did not smile as Arabella showed Beadle back out and guided him to a sofa in the tiny front parlour.

Time had been kind to her, Beadle thought. Though approaching fifty, she still possessed some of the vitality of complexion he remembered from her youth. He wondered if that was due to never having married.

Arabella perched on the adjacent sofa, but no sooner had she sat than she stood again. 'I'll fetch your tea.'

Perhaps she wanted to allay the fears of her friends. Would they think she was a police informer, like Joe Rees? That she was passing on the suffragist campaign activities to the authorities.

Flustered, he wondered if he too had blushed. The thing was, he just wasn't very confident around people who had been involved in an old case.

Nothing could be worse than death, of course, although

the dead were at least, one hoped, at peace with the Lord. Those who had been in the clutches of a murderer, felt his fingers on their skin, his knife at their throat, smelled his stinking breath, there was no treatment for them. They were left to live out their remaining days knowing that Death had held them. His bony fingers still clutched at their ankles, dragging them back to the grave.

In some ways, they were the living dead.

But no one thought of their trauma. All considered them lucky. But Beadle, whenever he had cause to see them – and he did not seek them out – saw it written in their harried eyes.

Beside him on a drum table sat a pile of pamphlets. *The Forerunner, Woman's Journal, Votes for Women*. A handbill for a reading by Arthur Conan Doyle at Cornish Brothers booksellers, tonight. Was Conan Doyle coming back to Moseley? No, not the Moseley village shop. The New Street store. But he was here in the city. Tonight. How curious.

Beadle checked the bookshelf. Volumes of *Sherlock Holmes*. The public's obsession with bloody gentleman detectives. But she also had leather bound volumes of Austen, the Brontës, Melville, H.G. Wells, and Oscar Wilde.

Life had been reasonably kind to Arabella Palmer, which was good, in view of what she had suffered. She was a successful woman, teacher, political pioneer, and she would not want reminding of the past.

He wished he hadn't come.

She bustled through with a cup of tea on a pewter platter. He fiddled with pouring milk and adding sugar, wishing he had refused; thinking he might knock the milk jug over. His hulking frame was too big for this room, for this china tea set.

Arabella Palmer perched on the chair across from him, her delicate hands curled in her lap, her back straight.

'I'm sorry that I called,' he said. 'I have interrupted your meeting.'

'We are rather used to our activities being disrupted by the police,' she said.

'And I assure you I have no interest in your activities. At least, professionally. You have nothing to fear from that.'

'It is at the hands of your profession that women from our movement are this minute being force-fed in Winson Green Prison. You have just met a woman who has suffered this torture.'

Bertha Ryland. He remembered her now from police photographs.

He sighed and sipped his tea. This wasn't going how he'd imagined. He had faced down murderers and the most vicious criminals Birmingham had to offer, but a room full of suffragettes made his stomach turn.

'I would hope,' he said, 'that the last time we crossed paths, it was my profession that protected you.'

She looked at her fingers, twisting a handkerchief in knots. 'It was not the law that saved me from the hands of a murderer,' she said. 'Not entirely.'

'And this, I regret to say, is the reason for my visit.'

'After twenty-four years, you come with news?'

'He was seen. Yesterday.'

She gripped the frilled collar at her throat. 'Who?'

'Pearce,' he said. 'Daniel Pearce.'

She heaved a sigh of relief.

'I have had a report of his appearance. In Moseley. Though the report is a little flimsy. The man who was seen bore a striking resemblance. Although it was said he looked younger.'

'Younger? I don't understand.'

'It was the considered opinion of the witness that the man in question might not be Daniel Pearce, but his son.' His eyes went to the bookshelf. 'Unless, of course, the works of H. G. Wells have more truth to them than we know.'

He smiled, but it was a poor joke. Arabella Palmer was not laughing.

'Why would his son concern me?' she said.

'It wouldn't, of course. I meant no offence.'

'Then what do you want from me?'

He put his teacup to one side, reached for his hat, and stood. 'I came to see if you had seen him; if he had made contact with you. I can see that is not the case.'

Arabella looked up at him with eyes glinting tears. 'Why on earth would he come to see *me?*'

'You seem to forget, madam, that Daniel Pearce was a murder suspect in an unsolved case.'

'You know as well as I do that it wasn't him.'

'None us of know. We are all left in the dark, with our doubts.'

He walked out to the hall and didn't care if she showed him out or not. The women in the back parlour stopped talking to listen. He had opened the front door and stepped out when he turned to find Arabella right behind him.

'I know you can't see it,' she said, 'but I believe Daniel Pearce saved me from that murderer.'

'I believe that too,' he said. 'But his disappearance left many questions unanswered. And what happened so soon afterwards… well, it haunts me, Miss Palmer. It should haunt us all.'

Again, the hand to her throat.

Beadle put on a smile. 'I noticed the handbill for the talk by Mr Conan Doyle tonight. Are you going?'

She looked down at her feet. 'I don't think it would be appropriate. He has said all he needs to say.'

'Mr Conan Doyle paints a very inaccurate picture of crime fighting,' Beadle said, as jovially as he could. 'Still, quite a coincidence. Both of them back here at the same time, what?'

He tipped his hat and edged around the garden gate with just one look back.

Nothing. Daniel Pearce had not made with her contact yet. If he had, it would be written all over her face. And there was nothing on Arabella Palmer's face but the ghosts of bad memories.

— 20 —

Danny got off the bus at Moseley village and Rachel followed him across the green.

'She's good looking, isn't she?'

'What does that have to do with it?

'If she was a minger you wouldn't be thinking of saving her.'

He turned, offended. 'Rachel, a girl is going to be murdered and we have the ability to prevent it and all you can say is it's because I fancy her?'

She laughed suddenly, not even listening. 'Look. We were right here. Last night. A hundred years ago.'

He looked around at it all with her. Moseley village as it was today, remembering how it had been last night in the gaslight gloom.

'Yeah,' he said. 'It's bizarre.'

'Do you keep thinking it's not real?'

'Then or now?' he said.

He didn't know anymore. Then seemed more real than this. He saw Amy Parker's green eyes and remembered how he couldn't take his own eyes from hers. He remembered how soft her hand felt when he'd reached out to shake it. He'd thought of little else n the last 24 hours.

They walked up the village to Buygones, the junk shop

next to the Prince of Wales pub, and stepped inside. It was a pirate's cave of objet d'arts and old tat, with a strong 1930s retro feel. The owner, Mitch, was a guy in his forties who dressed in 1930s casual, his moustache waxed up into points. He had a cravat on and a waistcoat and armbands on his shirtsleeves. He was even pouring tea from an art deco teapot and eating from a plate of cucumber sandwiches, cut into triangles. The only anomaly was the laptop on his wooden counter.

'Hi,' said Danny, putting on his posh voice. 'I wonder if you can help. We're looking for…'

Mitch held up a finger while he finished pouring.

'Tea?' he said.

'I'm sorry?'

'I can't drink it all myself.'

'Er, no. Thanks. Do you do coins?'

'I don't want tea either, thank you,' said Rachel.

'Old coins,' said Danny. '1912 if you've got any.'

Mitch measured him up for a beat. '1912, eh?'

'If you have any.'

'It's your lucky day,' he said, and pulled out a presentation pack of mint condition coins from under the counter. Danny took it and admired them.

'Full set,' said Mitch. 'Farthing, ha'penny, penny, threepence, sixpence, shilling, the florin… And a half crown.'

'How much are these?'

'Fifty quid.'

'What?' cried Rachel. 'There's only about a pound there.'

'Actually,' said Mitch. 'There's less than a pound. Your halfcrown is thirty pence, florin's twenty-four, shilling's twelve pence and the rest make a grand total of… seventy-six and three-quarter pence.'

'So nearly a quid then,' said Danny.

'Not even close,' said Mitch, who was enjoying himself much more than an explanation of old coins merited. 'There were two hundred and forty pence to the old pound.'

Rachel rolled her eyes.

'And this seventy-seven pence,' said Danny.

'Seventy-six and three-quarters.'

'That's fifty quid in today's money?'

'No way,' said Mitch. 'But these are. They're collector's items. Mint condition.'

Rachel took charge. 'Fascinating as this is,' she said. 'Do you have any *not* mint coins that collectors *aren't* interested in?'

Mitch sighed and pulled out a grubby old Oxo tin full of dirty coins and plonked it on the counter with a clatter.

'In there.'

'Okay,' said Rachel. 'See you.' She turned and headed for the door.

'Where are you going?' asked Danny.

'To get dressed,' she said. She walked out, the door chiming after her, and Danny started rooting through the coins, checking the dates. He looked up at Mitch.

'Do you have any notes as well?'

— 21 —

Danny walked into Mrs Hudson's dark and dingy vintage clothes shop, rattling his 1912 change in his pocket. He had managed to buy a small pile of coins and a few absurdly large banknotes for less than a tenner, and Mitch had assured him they amounted to the monthly wage of an average middle class head of household.

The shop had that smell he hated; the smell you got in charity shops: dead people's clothes and stale perfume. He saw a Ruritanian military jacket and took it off the rack and held it up against him to the mirror, admiring himself.

'That's not the year you're looking for.'

He turned, startled. Mrs Hudson was about 70 but there was something in her eyes that appeared younger, and stronger. She didn't smile and Danny felt suddenly uneasy under her gaze.

'You'd look very out of place in 1912 wearing that,' she said.

A long silence. How did she know?

Rachel bustled out of the changing room in a tweed walking suit.

'Oh my god, it's so heavy. How did they walk around in this!' She saw Danny and struck a pose. 'Well?'

'Er… Yeah. That looks great.'

He looked back at Mrs Hudson. She picked up a gentleman's suit that was draped over the counter and brought it over to him.

'Now for you,' she said. 'This, I think. Much less… conspicuous.'

He took the suit and sidled to the fitting room, relieved to escape the old woman's glare. It was like she'd looked right through him and seen everything he was thinking. He threw the suit on and admired himself in the mirror. He looked rather dashing, if he did say so himself, and he realized something that surprised him: he wanted to make a good impression on Amy Parker when he saw her next.

— 22 —

After Beadle's visit, the meeting continued. Arabella tried to brush aside their questions, but she could see that her suffragist comrades might suspect her of being an *agent provocateur,* so she came out with it: the whole sorry episode from twenty-four years ago.

She had been running ever since, running to stand still. She had run so that this would never define her. But here it was, all these years later, still haunting her waking moments.

Seeing that they would talk about this all day, she told them it was something she wished to forget and turned the matter back to their campaigning.

For an hour, she lost herself in a discussion of the growing militancy of the movement. Holding polite public meetings and smashing windows in London was not enough anymore; now the talk was of setting fire to post boxes and buildings, bombing a canal. Bertha had an idea to walk into Birmingham Art Gallery and slash a valuable painting.

They debated this for an hour. Could they countenance destroying a work of art? Bertha made an impassioned speech about her own mother's campaign to bring art to the working classes, but a society whose government denied women the vote, and imprisoned, force-fed and drugged them when they protested, was not a civilisation at all. What's more, it was a civilisation whose free press attacked its own women and portrayed them as sub-human. This 'civilisation' did not deserve fine art.

When they had gone, she stood in the front room, where Inspector Beadle had sat, staring at the hawthorn bush and the sparrows feeding on its berries, her mind in a whirl.

She must have stood frozen like that for an hour, for she came to, suddenly aware that she had been in a trance, and had long ago stopped thinking of bombing public buildings, but had been thinking of Daniel Pearce.

She ran up the stairs and emptied the great blue tea chest that looked like it might contain a pirate's hoard of treasure, but was packed with bed linen and old clothes. At the bottom, wrapped in muslin, was a sketchbook.

The one thing of Daniel Pearce's she had saved.

Slumped on the floor, against her bed, she flipped the pages. Haunting, lurid dream sketches. She had remembered being distraught at his graphic, violent paintings of nudes. They had seemed obscene at the time, though in her memory not so much now.

These sketches, though, were disquieting for an altogether different reason. The feverish imaginings of a disturbed mind, they seemed to be frantic, obsessive drawings of fantastical figures: a man who could summon up hurricanes and destroy cities; a red-haired woman swooping from the sky like an avenging harpy; a brown-haired girl with stars in her eyes standing by a gravestone, which was clearly St Mary's churchyard.

The scariest: a man who looked rather like Daniel, standing on a train platform, wearing a bowler hat, pointing a pistol at a clock, and fading from sight, so that he was half-transparent.

Scribbled along the side, the words, *Young and erring travellers we, All our dangers do not know.*

She knew the words. Yes, from a book she'd had as a girl.

A Religious Tract Society novel forced on her by her father. *Milly's Trials and Triumphs*. It had been designed to terrify young girls into following the ways of God. What a failure it had been. She remembered Daniel Pearce had been obsessed with the line.

Young and erring travellers we, All our dangers do not know.

Hot, woozy, as if the pages had infected her, she reached under the bed for the chamber pot and retched up the undigested tea and cakes of the afternoon meeting.

Emptying it out in the privy at the bottom of the garden, she wondered at Inspector Beadle's insinuation. She had suffered a profound trauma and her recollection of that fateful night was unclear.

Could Daniel have been a murderer?

This person she was, Arabella Palmer, was supposed to have died. Daniel had saved her life twice over, she was sure.

Some nights she felt that she did not belong on this Earth. What would happen if one saved a life that was destined not to be? What catastrophe might that unleash on the world?

She threw on her long coat and broad, ostrich feathered hat and marched down the street, the cold air bringing colour to her.

She had crested the hill of School Road before she thought of where she was going. But of course, it was obvious. There was only one place to go.

Turning into Oxford Road, she saw the spire of St Mary's through the bare trees, then realized, no, it wasn't. St Mary's didn't have a spire. It was the Baptist Church they had built the year he had disappeared. Once she was walking past it, she could see the crenulated battlements of St. Mary's. At the entrance to the Botanical Gardens on the corner, she crossed the road and marched through the lychgate, taking the path round to the graveyard.

At the corner of the church, she avoided a certain

flagstone. It had always sent a shudder through her, as if someone had walked over her grave. She skirted it and came out to the spacious vista of the churchyard.

This was where he had always come. It was a place that had seemed to fascinate him. She took the first path along the rear of the church building, passing a freshly dug grave, not stopping, breathless, as if some invisible force were pulling her to the spot at the lower end.

That grave, shaped like a child's cot. The one he was always drawn to. Something about it that had always fascinated him.

She halted, catching her breath, some twenty yards from the gravestone. Looking around, she expected to see him, coming to her through the tombstones. A phantom come at dusk to take her soul.

The air hummed, pregnant with summer storm static. She had seen no flash of lightning, but cowered anyway from a thunderclap she expected to crash over her head any moment.

Then the air around the gravestone seemed to fold in on itself and pop. She shrank behind a tall granite monument in the shape of Cleopatra's needle. Two people stood beside the gravestone. A man and a woman. Arabella checked around. She hadn't seen them enter. Where could they possibly have sprung from?

She peered from behind the needle.

Daniel.

She shouted his name in a silent scream.

They did not hear, but skulked away, through the wrought-iron gate and down the alleyway that led to the village green.

Her knees buckled and she slid down, her skirts ballooning around her. As she wept, slumped in the cold grass, she thought of a book she had at home. It was Oscar Wilde's *The Picture of Dorian Gray*.

It was him. She knew it.

But it was not the man she had almost married, but the Daniel from that day when, only ten years' old, she had first set eyes on him.

— 23 —

Rachel and Danny walked gingerly through the churchyard, awkward in their costumes, hoping no one would be around to see them. They'd both covered up with overcoats so they didn't look too strange on the way to the church and had their hats in carrier bags.

'Do you think she believed us, about making a student film?' said Danny. 'There was something funny about her.'

'Funny? She didn't crack a smile once.'

'I don't like her,' Danny muttered.

'Even after she gave you a discount.'

They reached the gravestone and took their hats out of their bags, put them on, took off their overcoats and stuffed them into the bags. Danny shoved both carrier bags under a nearby bush.

Rachel glanced around making sure no one could see them: two Edwardians standing in the local churchyard at night. She tried not to laugh when she thought they'd probably make anyone think they were seeing ghosts.

'Okay,' said Danny. 'Let's do it.'

They were through to the other side in an instant, still amazed at the sharp contrast in background noise.

There was no drunk there this time. The churchyard was as empty as it was in the present, a hundred years from now.

They pushed through the creaking wrought-iron gate and she noticed for the first time that it was cleaner in this year. She hadn't noticed it the first time. They walked swiftly down the dark space of the alley, to the door of light at the end.

They emerged from behind the billboard onto the green and stood, looking around in wonder at it all.

A busy crossroads with its Edwardian throng, horse-drawn carriages rolling this way and that, a line of carriages pulled up by the cabman's shelter, the horses silent, brooding. The electric tram sailed through the crossroads, heading for the city.

No one looked at them. They were right at home. Danny held out his arm and Rachel wondered what he was doing.

'Take my arm,' he said.

'Oh.' She slipped her hand in the crook of his arm and they set off up the street.

The Fighting Cocks pub looked exactly the same but the further up they walked, the more the buildings changed. The bookmakers on the corner was a grocer's. Where the two supermarkets now stood were a row of imposing Victorian redbrick shops with their wares out on the street and colourful hand-painted signs with ornate designs. They passed a fishmonger, a baker, a tiny WH Smith's newspaper agents, a watchmaker, a linen draper, another greengrocer, a china and glass dealer, a boot maker, and then they saw that Lloyds Bank was still there on the corner.

They crossed Woodbridge Road and admired the imposing Shufflebotham's Stores on the corner with the turret above and a fleet of carts outside. As they walked past more shops, Rachel couldn't help but stare at the people: a man with the most enormous set of bright red whiskers, wearing a cricket cap; a lady with a pale face and velvet dress who held a handkerchief to her nose; a one-legged old soldier with a grey beard holding out his military cap. Danny threw a coin in there and the old man nodded and croaked

'Thank you. God bless you, sir.'

Danny looked embarrassed, not at all the smug expression she'd expected. She squeezed his arm and then regretted it.

They walked past the Prince of Wales pub and on over the crest of the hill and began to descend down to Balsall Heath. Everything was so different she now realized, even though they were the same streets. Most of the houses were different, the paving stones on the pavement were different, the drainage grids, the pavements were lower, the kerbs smaller, more rounded, the road surface rougher, the road markings, the lamp posts, the lack of road signs; nothing was the same and if nothing was the same, how could it be the same place?

Danny crossed over to the other side and she didn't ask why, just went with him. He seemed to have a plan of some sort. They walked on and he eventually stopped a hundred yards short of the Brighton Road crossroads, beyond which the street seemed to thicken with life, hazy in the distance, as if further on, Balsall Heath seethed with anger.

Danny nodded at a terraced house across the road.

'That's where she lives.'

She stared and tried to imagine how many people had lived there in the past hundred years and wondered who lived there now, back in her present.

'I've walked past this so many times,' she said.

'I know. Too weird.'

'So, what's the plan?'

'I've no idea,' he said.

He looked at a loss and she was disappointed in him for the first time. She'd thought he'd have it all worked out and know what to do.

'You must have thought of something. We're here now.'

'All right then,' he said. 'I'll knock on the door and say "Hello, Mr Parker. Your daughter's going to be murdered on Saturday and you're going to cark it in the loony bin next month, probably because it's you that killed her. Oh, did I mention I'm from the future?"'

A man passed, hunched over, cloth cap low.

'You might not want to mention that out loud,' she said.

'I need to talk to her, alone,' he said. 'Find out stuff.'

'Like what?'

'Like why she's so scared of her father.'

'Maybe she knows he's going to kill her.'

'No,' he said. 'It wasn't that. It was something else.'

'Look!' She pointed up the street. 'It's the electric tram.'

It came speeding past them, faster than she thought it could ever travel, then slowed abruptly and stopped a hundred yards away.

'I wish we had trams still,' she said. 'They're so much better than the buses.'

Danny was looking back at the house. 'I'm going to go round the back. Try and talk to her. You stay here, keep an eye out.'

'Okay. I'll phone you if anything happens.'

He looked at her like she'd escaped from the loony bin herself.

'What?' she said.

'Rachel. Seeing as the mobile phone mast won't be built for another ninety years, I don't think you're going to get much of a signal.'

She reddened. 'I was joking,' she said, hoping he'd believe her. She watched him cross the road and walk up a side street a few doors away.

— 24 —

Danny walked round to the rear of the row of houses, which were all fenced at the back. The side street revealed a tree-lined square behind the houses, with a single gaslamp casting an eerie glow. It seemed a square that was an afterthought. No one came here to walk, it was too small for that. No houses looked onto it. It was a sullen patch of grass edged with trees that was destined to be developed into houses one day, because this forgotten patch of land was taking up valuable space.

He counted off the chimney stacks along the row till he came to what must have been the rear of number 12, and peered over the chest high wooden fence, looking up at the windows of the house.

A figure was at one of the rear windows – a woman, gazing out across the gloom, her face resting on her fist. He recognized her immediately, his mind flooding with memories of their brief encounter. Glancing around, he waved, but she didn't stir. She couldn't see him in the dark.

After a minute or more, she disappeared from the window and he breathed again. He looked around in panic for some small stones, scooped some up from the grass verge and threw the first at the window. The first four missed and slapped the wall. The fourth hit the window with a dull crack.

He cringed, aware he was in danger of smashing the window.

Amy came to the window again, peering out curiously.

He waved and wondered if she would be scared and call her father.

She waved back.

In a moment, he'd skipped over the fence and padded down the garden. Her window was above the outhouse and he scooted up the drainpipe. She opened her window as he stood up to face her.

'Hello, Amy Parker,' he grinned, panting from the sudden exertion.

'What are you doing here?' she whispered.

'I came to see you. To talk.'

'I'll be in frightful trouble if my father sees you.'

He frowned. How was he going to explain this to her? She would never believe him if he told her. 'Is your father ill?'

'Why do you ask that? You're a very forward man, Danny Pearce.'

'Do you mind that?'

She smiled for the first time. 'No. I should, but I don't. Why is that?'

'Because you like me?'

'I'm sure I don't even know you.'

It was true, and he had more important things to tell her, but he couldn't help feeling drunk in her presence.

'And I don't know *you,*' he said. 'But I feel like I do.'

'Yes. Yes, that's exactly how it feels. It's very odd.' She looked back at her bedroom door. 'Can you come back again? On Saturday?'

'Saturday,' he said. He had no idea what time she would be murdered on Saturday. 'That's too late.'

She frowned again. 'I have the oddest sensation when I see you.'

'What is it?'

'I can't describe it. The other day, at Mr Rieper's funeral, when I first saw you. It was as if you'd travelled a thousand miles, just to see me.'

He took her emotion eagerly, as if it were a love letter. 'Yes. I felt that too.'

'What does it mean?' she said.

He had an idea. 'What if I'd been sent here, somehow, to protect you.'

'From what?' she said, but he could see in her eyes that she already suspected it herself.

'Yes. What if something terrible was going to happen and I was sent here to stop it happening?'

'Don't be silly.'

He reached out and touched her hands, resting on the window sill. 'You feel it too. I can tell.'

She flinched with sudden panic and looked behind at a sound. 'You can't stay here. Come again, Saturday.'

She went to close the window.

'Wait,' he said. He took out his phone.

'What's that?' she said.

'It's a camera. Stay still.' He snapped her.

'You're playing a silly joke on me, Danny Pearce. I've a good mind not to speak to you at all.' She closed the window and shooed him away.

'You have to,' he said.

She put her hand to the window pane and he placed his own against it. Her eyes were full of fear and wonder. Yes, something bad was going to happen. She knew it. He watched her walk back across her room and disappear into the house.

He jumped down off the outhouse roof and crouched against it, looking at his phone and the shadowy image on the screen: Amy Parker's ghostly face.

— 25 —

Rachel loitered on the corner, trying not to look shifty, standing just outside the pool of light offered by the nearest gaslamp. It gave off enough light for her to see, but she was in shadow.

A few people passed by: a man who tipped his hat to her, which she thought was sweet; another who ignored her, which was disappointing; and a couple, the woman averting her eyes, the man shooting her a dirty look. She wondered if there was something about her costume that was inappropriate. The dress was a good length, she wasn't showing any ankle, and it had a high collar so her neck was hidden. She thought she looked quite staid, but knew it was an era where showing your knees would be the same as walking topless down the high street.

A labourer sauntered towards her in rough, plaster-coated overalls and heavy boots, slumped and exhausted from what must have been a backbreaking day of work. She watched him closely, taking in every detail of his clothing, fascinated, and glanced up at his eyes, which shone a piercing bright blue from his dirty face. He lifted his cloth cap. She nodded.

He passed. Then he stopped and turned.

'Even,' he said.

She was confused for a moment, then realized he'd

mumbled a *good evening* to her.

'Hello,' she answered, looking around to see if anyone else was on the street. They were pretty much alone.

'Cold night for it,' he said.

'I'm warm enough, thank you.'

He looked up and down the street and a chill settled on her heart. He stroked his chin and she heard the crackle of his stubble.

'How much a turn?' he mumbled.

'I'm sorry?'

'How much?'

'You what?' She was looking over his shoulder now at the side street that Danny had gone down, desperately hoping he would appear.

'I've got a florin for it,' he said. 'Where's your nest?' He took her arm and started to shove her off the street. 'Come on, darling, let's not hang around.'

'Get off me!' she wailed, but her voice caught in her throat and it came out as a strangled cry that no one heard. She hit out at him, swiping him on the nose.

He pulled away, shocked, glaring.

'Do one,' she spat, with sudden venom. 'Now!'

The menace in his face turned to confusion. This wasn't what he was used to. There was something very different about this girl. He backed away and his confusion turned to anger as he scampered off, spitting out a last retort. 'You little bitch.'

She caught her breath, realising how nasty it had almost been and was still gasping when Danny emerged from the side street and crossed the road to join her.

'I'm gonna kill that Mrs Hudson,' she said. 'She's given me a 1912 tart's outfit. I've had all sorts asking me how much.'

Danny didn't seem surprised. 'Well, we *are* on the edge of the old red light district,' he said. 'In fact, it was a big area for prostitution until recently.'

'Oh, thanks. You're a real gent.' She noticed movement over his shoulder. 'Is that him?'

A gentleman had emerged from the front door of number 12 and was walking down the garden path, wearing a top hat and black overcoat. She could see a shock of blonde beard. He opened the gate and crossed to their side of the street and strolled north, heading towards the city.

'That's Parker,' said Danny. 'Come on. Let's follow.'

Rachel dragged him back. 'Why?'

'Because I think he's our murder suspect.'

— 26 —

All day, Joe Rees had waited for movement in the alley, his heart jumping every time someone came out. He had barely looked a customer in the eye as they bought their papers, always looking over their shoulders.

One of his regulars had remarked on it. 'Are you all right, Joe?'

'What's that?'

'You don't seem all here, Joe.'

'Aw,' he said, taking his eyes off the gap between the row of shops on the other side. 'Got a touch of the old collywobbles, today. Someone dancing on my grave.'

'You finish early and get yourself home to a nice, warm bed.'

He hadn't done that, he thought, Not ever. No day off sick, no holiday. Not once in forty years. Selling papers here day in, day out. He was as much a feature on the green as the bull's head up there above the door of the pub.

The light was falling and the traffic thickening, trams from the city more frequent, dropping off commuters who picked up the evening edition on the way home.

That was when he came.

This time it was Daniel Pearce. There was no mistaking it.

He was dressed in an out-of-fashion suit that looked baggy

on him, but not as strange as he'd looked the first time, with no hat and looking like he was wearing farmer's clothes or a convict's garb.

He was with a woman. Yes, she'd been with him the first time, and he remembered now how strange it was that they'd appeared from the mouth of the alley that led up to the churchyard, looked at the newspapers and then gone straight back the way they'd come.

He'd forgotten to mention that detail to Inspector Beadle. He would have to remember it next time he reported to him. Joe had always been one for detail – which was why he'd been such a good police informer. He'd have to keep a sharp eye on things now he was back in business.

Daniel Pearce and the girl looked around them and took it all in, and then they turned right.

Joe took the money off his customer and said, 'Sorry, I'm closing shop.'

He had thrown his pile of papers inside and locked the cabin before his customers could object. Money lost, and they'd go to W. H. Smiths forevermore, but that might be offset by what Beadle would pay.

The couple were well up the street before he was following, jogging at first till he was ten yards behind.

Don't let him see you, he thought. He could be dangerous.

The girl was holding onto his arm now. Who was she?

Cursing as he passed the WH Smith's shop, he glanced at the array of clock faces in the watchmaker's window and felt a shudder of something not quite right.

They crossed the street and looked like they might be about to walk into Shufflebotham's, but they carried on.

Daniel threw a coin into Old Corporal Cooper's hat and you could tell he'd done it to impress the girl because she pulled him in a bit closer.

The foot traffic thinned out as they passed the Prince of

Wales and Joe slowed down. He could keep them in sight from further back. There was no chance of losing them, not with the road so straight for a while.

The girl was looking around at everything like she was on holiday in a strange, new place. Maybe she was a stranger here. That was why he'd never seen her before. Daniel looked on ahead. That was an important difference. He would make a note of it. These little details were why he was the best informer in the business.

Down the gentle hill as they left Moseley and headed towards Balsall Heath, Daniel suddenly pulled her to one side and they crossed the road. Joe waited for a tram to rattle past and nipped across behind it, so they wouldn't look back and see him cross.

A good thirty yards behind them now, he was surprised when they suddenly stopped. Joe carried on walking as slowly as he could but he was almost pin-heading and it would look out of place. He stopped and pulled tobacco from his pocket and rolled a cigarette, keeping one eye on them as he did. They were talking and seemed interested in a house across the street – one of the swanky big town houses in that row.

Joe walked on. If he stood watching them much longer, he would draw attention to himself. Lowering his hat over his face, he quickened his step and edged past them. They were deep in conversation and didn't notice him at all.

This was the curious thing. Daniel did not recognize Joe. So how could it be him?

He'd only caught a flash of the conversation, Hardly anything at all, but the name *Parker* had stood out. And the word *murder*, and just as he'd brushed past them and smelled a curious waft of some exotic, aromatic perfume, the words *it's you that killed her*. Then something about the future.

His mind racing, and wishing he had a notepad and pencil to write all of this down, he stopped at the tram stop and looked back just as Daniel crossed the street and disappeared into a side street. Louise Lorne Road.

He'd left the girl on the other side.

What to do?

It was too risky to run back and follow Daniel. What if he smacked right bang into him as came back out? No. The girl was watching a house, and Daniel was going round the back.

Perhaps they were going to burgle a place.

He decided to cut around. He crossed and marched down Trafalgar Road and took the bend that ran parallel to the main road. He cut in at the other end of Louise Lorne Road and slowed, fearing he might run headlong into Daniel.

The suspect. The murderer.

He edged down the back street, coming into a close where the backs of the houses met. He became aware that he was wheezing. Not as young as he used to be. Perhaps he really was too old for this, and that was why Beadle had let him go. The inspector had been embarrassed to see him again, that was clear. Perhaps he had hired him again out of pity. Well, he'd show him. He had proof that Daniel Pearce was planning a murder, and he might just be able to tell him who the victim was, before it had even happened.

Wouldn't that be a feather in the old cap for Joe Rees, and no mistake?

There was no sight of Daniel Pearce. He must have gone back.

Joe edged around till he could see right up Louise Lorne Road through to the street. The girl was still standing there on the corner. A man was with her. But it wasn't Daniel Pearce. Some labourer. No wonder, what with her hanging around on street corners like a common giggler.

He looked back over the empty close. Where had he gone?

Then it caught his eye, the one unusual thing across the row of houses: a man standing on an outhouse, at a back window. Was he breaking in?

No. A girl at the window. Talking. A secret meeting.

Romeo and Juliet. Wasn't there a lot of murder in that play as well? Love and murder. Perhaps Daniel Pearce and this girl were plotting to kill her husband. No. She looked too young from this distance. Nothing but a girl. Her father then.

This was more information than he thought he could ever have gleaned. Inspector Beadle's jaw would drop onto his desk when old Joe Rees told him all of this.

The girl closed the window and they pressed their palms to the glass. They were definitely secret lovers. Skulking round the old back entrance too. Daniel Pearce jumped down to the garden. Joe skulked behind a lamppost and peeped out.

He came over the fence with the bounce of a young man and scooted off to join the girl out front.

Joe counted the back gates along the row of houses and followed.

They were talking on the street corner. He would have to decide which way to turn when he reached the end of the side street. Either way, he would have his back to them and wouldn't be able to watch them.

But just as he came to the mouth of the street, they turned and walked off towards the city. They had their eyes on a gent in a top hat who had just crossed the street to their side. Was it this Parker fellow they were planning to murder? Had he just come from the house, not realising the tryst that had occurred at the rear of his own house. Literally behind his back?

The dirty, low scoundrels.

The gent stopped at the tram stop and the murderous couple followed and joined him there.

A tram came trundling from Moseley village.

He couldn't follow them. It was too close now. He let the tram scoop them up and take them away.

Walking along the row of villas, he counted the houses till he came to number 12. He pushed the gate open and walked up the long front garden to the door and pressed the bell.

A girl came to the door. No servant. He filed that information away, thinking it might be useful later.

Sweeping off his cloth cap, he put on his harmless old man voice. 'Oh, good evening to you, young lady. I was after calling on Mr Parker. Only I can't be at all sure I have the right house. It is Mr Parker's residence, isn't it?'

The girl assessed him coolly. She was a devious bugger and no mistake. Clear blue eyes and a haughty demeanour. Stuck up. She wasn't a girl at all, but in the full bloom of early womanhood. And already scheming and plotting. Such was the fairer sex.

'And who would like to know?'

'Joseph Rees. Friend of your father, is it?'

'I'm sure he's never mentioned a Joseph Rees before and I'm sure I've never seen you.'

'I've entered into a business discussion with Mr Parker,' Joe said.

'Wait. I have seen you,' she said. 'You sell the newspapers on the village green.'

'That's right. Your father discussed me supplying his business on a long-term contract.'

The girl wavered, thinking it through. 'He's not here. You just missed him.'

'Ah, what a misfortune, madam. Might I ask where he's gone? I might catch him up.'

'I couldn't tell. Nor would I.'

Joe smiled and bowed his head. 'Then I shall catch him another time. Thank you for your kindness, miss.'

He put his hat back on and turned, not looking back, and only hearing the door slam shut when he was ten yards up the street.

He quickened his step. The police station was five minutes away. He had to tell Beadle everything before he forgot it.

— 27 —

Danny and Rachel set off to follow but were immediately taken by surprise when Mr Parker stopped walking and stood at the tram stop opposite the tram depot only a hundred yards from his house.

They slowed, wondering what to do, then heard the tram rumbling behind them, roaring down the slope from the village.

Danny quickened his pace. 'He's getting the tram.'

'We're not getting it with him, are we?'

'Why not?'

'Too scary.'

'You said you liked the tram.'

She pulled him back, her feet rooted with fear. 'Wandering around 1912 Moseley is one thing, Danny, but setting out to other parts of the city... no way.'

The entire city of Birmingham was out there – its great, sprawling, dangerous mass – and it made her long to be within touching distance of that gravestone in St Mary's churchyard.

'Well, I'm going,' he said, shaking her off and striding for the tram stop.

Rachel looked back up the street as the tram roared past. The dark rise to Moseley was lit by pools of gaslight. But between here and St Marys were so many shadows.

She ran for the stop, where the electric tram screeched to a halt. Mr Parker was cloaked in a thick cloud of cigar smoke. Danny took her hand and stepped onto the rear platform. Mr Parker had gone up the open stairs so they followed him to the upper deck. It was covered but the sides were open. They sat a few seats behind him, the smell of his cigar thick in their faces despite the absence of windows.

The tram set off again and wheezed through the Brighton Road crossroads, with its strange turreted building standing guard like a watchtower.

Rachel gazed out and noticed the street change character. It was as if, in crossing the Brighton Road, they'd not only crossed over from genteel Moseley into roughshod Balsall Heath, from the suburbs into the city, but also from respectability into debauchery. She'd studied the history of the two neighbourhoods and their dramatic differences, which survived on to her present. How Balsall Heath had always been the poor relation, defecting to the city twenty years before Moseley, which had tried to stay aloof, and how its red light reputation had existed up until the 1990s, when its growing Muslim population had driven it out. As the tram sailed down the Moseley Road, she could see it was nothing but a boulevard of gin houses and brothels.

A few stops further on they reached Highgate, and Balsall Heath suddenly seemed genteel. Highgate was a dingy slum with not even gin houses and brothels to give it some respectability. Mr Parker stood up and walked down the stairs. Rachel and Danny looked at each other with amazement.

'We have to,' said Danny.

Rachel groaned and followed him down the steep stairs.

They stepped off the tram after Mr Parker, who strode off, still puffing on his cigar. Rachel shuddered, feeling the danger of the place; it had a physical quality that polluted the air, like smog. It was dirty and smelly and the streets were crowded with shawled women carrying jugs of ale, men reeking of booze and sweat, wearing shabby clothes and scuffed boots. They hung around on corners, glaring at them with glassy eyes. Barefoot children wore rags that could barely be called clothes. Mr Parker looked out of place striding through it, and so did Rachel and Danny.

He turned into a shop and they both sighed with relief. When they reached it they realized it was a pharmacy.

'Should we go inside?' asked Rachel.

'He'd notice us. And I've no idea what to ask for.'

'I don't like it out here.'

'Me neither.'

She scanned the surroundings for a safe haven. There was a pub on the opposite corner but it looked like a hell hole: a mob of drinkers in peaked caps had piled out into the street outside, roaring, smoking, swearing, fighting. A young woman in a shawl came and pleaded with a man to come home, tried to drag him away, only to be punched and sent on her way with a farewell kick, which seemed to amuse the other men there who all cheered him on.

Rachel stared with horror. A few of the drinkers noticed them, glowering across the street. Some of them exchanged words and glanced back at them.

'I don't like this,' said Danny.

They goaded one of the young drinkers on and pushed him into the street. He made his way across to them, a glint in his eye.

Rachel knew this meant trouble and that she might stay rooted to the spot and let it all happen out of politeness rather than risk hurting his feelings by running away.

Danny snatched her hand and dragged her inside the shop, the bell ringing as they stepped inside. She heard a disappointed *Aaaaah!* rise up from the drinkers and knew they had escaped a beating.

There were a handful of people standing inside the pharmacy and a hush of respectability, as if they'd stepped into a library out of a riot. The walls were lined with jars of potions and an elderly, balding man behind the counter seemed to be the pharmacist. He was ushering Mr Parker through a door. She caught a glimpse of them both walking up a flight of stairs before the door closed behind them with its brass notice marked *Private*.

The pharmacist's assistant, a younger gentleman in a white smock, had taken over counter duty and was dispensing medicines in small vials and neatly wrapped paper parcels. They shuffled uncertainly as the customers were dealt with and left the shop one by one. Rachel peered out of the window through the gaps in the elegant bottles of blue and red liquid on display, and saw that the drinkers across the road had forgotten about them, more interested in the fist fight that was taking place in their midst.

She browsed the cabinets and displays and marvelled at the array of remedies: *Venos Lightning Cough Cure, Radium Hand Cleanser, Pettingill's Kidney-Wort Tablets, John Melrose Southern Counties Cream,* which was confusingly from Edinburgh, *Dr Blumer's Camphorated Oil, Puretest Tincture Iodine, Watson's Linseed Lozenges, California Syrup of Figs,* eucalyptus gums, Glauber salts, *Price's Epsom Salts, Beecham's Pills,* sulphur tablets, *Owbridges Lung Tonic, Hudson's Cherry Lincture.*

The last customer was served and the assistant turned to Danny.

'Yes, sir. How can I help you?'

Danny stammered. He had frozen and had no idea what to say.

'I have a terrible headache,' said Rachel, putting the back of her hand to her temple, a touch melodramatically. 'In fact, I feel quite faint.'

She swooned to her left, as close as possible to the wooden

chair. Danny caught her, real shock on his face, and let her sink onto it. The assistant rushed around to help her.

'I'm sorry,' she said. 'Please forgive me, it's nothing.'

'You stay there, Miss,' said the assistant. 'What is it you feel?'

'Just a tremendous headache,' she said. 'I don't know why I felt faint. I think it's just rather hot in here.'

The assistant rushed behind the counter to a sink to pour a glass of water.

Danny leaned in close to her. 'Are you okay?' he said.

'Of course I am,' she whispered. 'We just need some time.'

The assistant returned with the water and she sipped it down. The glass tumbler was heavy in her hand. She'd never felt a glass that thick.

'Now, for your headache, Miss,' he said.

'She'll be fine with some aspirin,' said Danny.

The assistant frowned. 'I could add some powder to the water,' he said. 'But I think some *Pinkham's Compound* would be better.'

Rachel shot Danny a warning glare.

'Well, yes, I suppose so,' he said. 'If you say so.'

The assistant went to one of the cabinets, which he opened with a key, and brought back a small bottle with brown liquid inside. He took out the cork stopper, poured the thick syrup into a teaspoon and offered it to Rachel. She looked at it uncertainly.

'This should set you right, Miss.'

She lipped it off the teaspoon and winced at the sharp taste of aniseed, the thick syrup coating her throat. The assistant handed her the bottle and she glanced at the mass of small type on the label. She could only make out *Lydia E. Pinkham's Vegetable Compound, for Prolapsus Uteri,* and lower down, *Female Weaknesses.*

'Thank you,' she gasped.

The door marked *Private* opened and Mr Parker came out,

followed by the pharmacist. Danny bent himself close over Rachel to hide both their faces as he passed them and left the shop, the bell above the door ringing.

'I feel much better now,' said Rachel.

'Yes, thank you,' said Danny.

'I won't wrap the bottle now you've opened it,' said the assistant, walking back behind the counter. 'That'll be fourpence, please sir.'

Danny fiddled with a handful of coins for an age before handing over the right money. He pocketed the bottle, tipped his hat and said goodbye, taking Rachel outside. They walked off briskly up the road, following Mr Parker, who was a good hundred yards ahead.

'Come on,' said Danny. 'He might get the tram back and we need to be on it.'

They marched down the gaslit street as fast as they could, ready to break into a run at the first sign of attention from the locals. As they emerged on the Moseley Road, the tram pulled up and Mr Parker stepped onto it. They ran the last few yards and jumped onto the rear platform as it pulled away. Danny was about to climb the stairs but Rachel pulled him into the lower deck.

'We can see when he gets off from here,' she said.

He followed her to a seat and they fell into it with relief.

The acrid taste of the medicine was still fetid in her throat. 'I think that medicine is going to make me sick. God knows what's in it.'

'It said *Vegetable Compound*. It's probably just some herbal remedy.'

'It said it's for *Female Weaknesses*. Didn't Queen Victoria take laudanum for that? Isn't that basically heroin?'

'You'll be all right,' he said.

The tram roared out of Highgate and headed back to civilisation. But unfortunately, before they could reach it, Mr Parker stepped off in Balsall Heath.

— 28 —

Inspector Beadle left the station earlier than his customary 7pm, and instead of heading straight for his empty Maypole home – devoid of life and warmth since the tragic death of his wife – he took a city-bound tram. It was almost empty, the trams full of human life all streaming past on the other side. Forever, it seemed, he was against the tide.

He arrived in the teeming gaslit city, unnerved by the sheer bustle of the throng. Each time he came it was more crowded than the last, as if it were a giant anthill spawning and spreading by the minute.

Birmingham had been a few respectable streets ringed by a giant slum for many years, but slowly the respectability had pushed the slums outwards till they now bordered the respectable suburbs. Peakies and sloggers had held sway here for decades, but they were now taking over that area they called the 'inner city'.

The city fathers had managed to push the poverty out of arms' reach so they didn't have to hold their noses anymore. It was the problem of the suburban police now.

He walked into Cornish Brothers booksellers on New Street, to find it buzzing with activity. Rows of chairs were laid out, and a desk piled with books, like an impromptu barricade that had been thrown up to protect the author from the marauding masses.

And there sat Arthur Conan Doyle.

His thick moustache was white now, and his eyes had become screwed up, but the flicker of intelligence was still bright. There was still something of the amateur sleuth about him – a busybody thinking he was smarter than the police whose job it was to catch real criminals, not sit on their backsides imagining what it would be like to do so.

Beadle stood at the back, leaning on a pillar.

A well-dressed reptilian looking gentleman who sat beside the famous author, stood and made a little speech, and told the audience that Arthur Conan Doyle would sign copies of his latest novel, *The Lost World*, and take questions on the fascinating issues of prehistory, spiritualism and theosophy, but would not discuss Sherlock Holmes.

Groans from the seated audience of ladies and gentlemen.

Conan Doyle stood and gave a little talk about how lovely it was to be back in Birmingham again after such a long time. He said a little about the serialisation of *The Lost World* in the Strand magazine. The publication of the novel had coincided fortuitously with his friend Charles Dawson unearthing a startling find regarding our prehistoric ancestry: the 'Piltdown Man' remains recently discovered in East Sussex.

Then he read a bit of his new book, which was some nonsense about dinosaurs that held the audience in thrall.

Beadle flinched as someone nudged him in the ribs. He looked into the clear blue eyes of Arabella Palmer.

He read the need in them, that she had been unable to resist being drawn back into the mystery that haunted them both.

— 29 —

Rachel and Danny jumped off the tram after Mr Parker and followed at a distance. He seemed to be walking the rest of the way home. She found herself thinking of movies she'd seen of *Jack the Ripper* or *Doctor Jekyll and Mr Hyde*, following a man in a top hat through the mist of a gaslit street that was an explosion of gin bars and brothels. Music and rowdiness bellowed from every single door, and women calling out to every man that passed, asking if he fancied some fun. But unlike those films, the women were not scantily-clad glamour girls caked in make-up; they were plain and tired, their faces bloated, eyes glassy. Their dresses and hats were flamboyant, with ruffles, feathers and brocade and as much cheap material to peacock them as they could muster, but there was no flesh on show at all. Their flouncy skirts went down to their boots and their lacy collars to their chins.

'Oh my god,' said Rachel. 'It's rougher than it is now!'

'Tell me about it,' said Danny.

He was looking quite uncomfortable at running the gauntlet of so much blatant solicitation and she felt his arm grip a little more tightly on her hand.

In Moseley, it had seemed that the chief forms of communication were the tipped hat and the handshake. Here it was more the shout of abuse and the punch up. They passed three fights taking place outside bars that no one else seemed to notice, and two of them were between rival prostitutes.

To their surprise, Mr Parker turned into one of the bars, a cluster of peak-capped young scarfaces stepping apart respectfully as he entered.

'He's gone in that bar,' said Danny. 'I can't believe it. It looks so *rough*.'

'Come on then. It's your round.'

'Do you think we should? I don't mind admitting it, but I'm actually scared now.'

Rachel grinned. Danny was so posh, he had no idea how to handle this. She had no idea either, but felt it should be more her element.

'We've got a murder to solve,' she said, pretending to be fearless. 'We're not going to find out anything here.'

They walked to the door and the gang of youths outside parted to let them through. Inside, through a thick pall of smoke, they found an eclectic mixture of roughs and toffs seated at scores of tables. A cabaret seemed to be taking place on a stage, but no one could hear it. The singer went through the motions but her song was drowned out by the shouts, screams and laughter of the customers.

Rachel and Danny hovered uncertainly, not knowing what to do. Mr Parker had somehow found a table to himself. A waiter who looked about fifteen years old breezed up to them.

'Evening, sir. I can fit you in stageside if you like?'

'Er, yeah. I mean, yes, thank you.'

The waiter led them through the crowd to the empty table next to Mr Parker's. They sat and Danny nodded to him. Mr Parker rose slightly from his seat for Rachel's benefit and tipped his hat.

'What'll it be, sir?' said the waiter.

'Er… Two V and T's?' said Danny.

'You what?'

Danny looked uncertain. He glanced around to see what

other people were drinking but they all had bottles he didn't recognize.

'The same as those,' he said.

'Gin spesh for two. Right away, sir.'

He rushed off.

A different waiter, younger than their own, rushed over to Mr Parker and left a bottle, pouring something ruby red into the glass. A fight broke out on the other side of the bar between two tarts. They got pushed out onto the street, a screaming ball of hair and rouge. All the men around them laughed riotously.

'I thought chavs were a new invention as well,' said Rachel.

Their waiter came back with a green bottle and two glasses. 'Here you are, sir. It's a bit quiet tonight, I'm afraid.'

Rachel looked aghast while he poured the gin.

'That's a florin, sir.'

Danny shuffled through the coins in his palm and handed him one. The waiter stayed with his hand held out.

'Oh yes,' said Danny, handing him another coin graciously. 'This is for you.'

The waiter looked at it like he'd spat in his palm. 'Your fortune went down with the Titanic, then?' He marched off, shaking his head.

'Danny Pearce, you cheapskate,' Rachel laughed.

'That'll be worth a tenner in a hundred years.'

Rachel watched the waiter go back to his bar and say something to a couple of shabby genteel men propped up against it. They looked over and checked out the new arrivals. One of them – glassy-eyed, trying to focus – looked familiar. She tried to place him.

Another fight broke out: two men punching the sweat off each other to general laughter.

'Okay, I admit it,' said Rachel. 'I'm scared too.'

Danny peeked over at Mr Parker, watching the stage and

seemingly oblivious to the carnage all around.

'Good evening, sir,' he said.

Mr Parker turned in his seat and inspected them but said nothing.

'It's quite a lively place,' said Danny with a nervous laugh.

Mr Parker seemed to think about it, then said, 'Lively. Live. As surely as I live, I will do to her the very things I heard you say.'

Danny nodded, not sure how to respond. He took a shot of his drink and gasped for air. Rachel did the same and her eyes bulged. Danny coughed and recovered, thumping his chest.

'Yeah,' he said. 'You live close by?'

He groaned as it came out of his mouth, and Rachel wondered if it was due to the gin or that he'd realized it was such an utterly useless line of enquiry.

Mr Parker leaned closer and fixed Danny with an intense, crazed gaze. 'Numbers fourteen eighteen,' he said. 'That's why she will be punished. For my sin.'

They stared.

Mr Parker looked away, completely normal again.

Over by the bar, Rachel saw the drunk collect himself and clench his fists, staring with glassy venom.

A prostitute came over and whispered in Mr Parker's ear. He rose from his chair, she picked up his bottle and glass and he followed her through the crowd and out of a side door. They caught a glimpse of him ascending the stairs with her before the door closed again.

'I think we better go now,' said Danny.

'But we still don't know if he's the one who kills her.'

'Oh, come on, Rachel. He's *insane*. Of course he kills her.'

'I'll kill *you*.'

They looked up at the drunk towering over them. Rachel recognized him at last. The drunk from the graveyard.

'Get up,' he snarled.

'I'm all right here, thank you,' said Danny.

'I said, get up!'

He swung a punch, his massive fist arcing in slow motion. Danny ducked in his seat. The drunk wheeled round, carried by the momentum of his fist, which smacked into the nearest sot.

'Oy!' the sot shouted.

The sot lamped the drunk and sent him flying against a crowd of inebriates. Almost instantly, the whole bar was fighting, tables and bottles flying.

'Let's go!' shouted Rachel.

She grabbed Danny's hand and tried to push through the pile of scrapping bodies to the door. But the graveyard drunk pulled Danny back.

'Where d'you think you're going!'

He threw another swipe. Danny ducked and threw his own punch with his eyes closed. His fist hit the drunk in the neck and sent him flying sideways, taking several fighters with him. They were free, almost near the door.

Danny turned, ready to run out of there, but another great big hand grabbed hold of him. It belonged to a great big police sergeant.

'You'll do!' he boomed. 'Come on!'

Danny's feet barely scraped the ground as the bear of a man carted him outside.

Rachel rushed after.

The police sergeant threw Danny into the back of a wagon. She watched helplessly as other policemen stormed in. They took a handful of fighters and threw them in the van with Danny, brushing off the screaming prostitutes.

She wanted to shout out, like them, but her throat was paralysed by fear.

The sergeant slapped the lock on the wagon and it jolted off into the night.

Danny had been arrested.

— 30 —

'Miss Palmer,' Inspector Beadle whispered. 'You haven't come to break windows, I take it?'

'What a low opinion you must have of me.'

'I wouldn't want to have to arrest you,' he said, trying to make light of it, and then was taken aback at the thought, the very real thrill of holding her. He shuddered as if to shake the feeling off, like a dog out of the rain, and forced himself to look at the famous author.

Arabella Palmer whispered in his ear. 'Shouldn't I long to see the great man of letters talk about this Piltdown Man, seeing as the Daily Express has now taken to calling every suffragette Piltdown *Woman?*'

She was bitter and distraught. His joke had fallen down a deep well, to echo a very lonely sounding splosh.

A woman in the back row glanced back with a spiteful glare. Beadle leaned in closer to Arabella Palmer, the scent of her skin intoxicating. It had been so long since he'd breathed in the scent of a woman. He was acutely aware that he was cast out from their society now. An ageing widower working his final days in monastic seclusion.

He wondered if he'd really sought her out over a case at all.

'Thankfully,' he said, 'we do not all take our opinions

from the Daily Express.'

Conan Doyle finished his reading to thunderous applause and then the lizard-looking chairman asked a few prepared questions: about his interest in spiritualism and why it had developed since 1888.

Beadle felt the back of his neck prickle at the date. When he was here last. When it all happened. The thing that dragged them all back, Beadle and Conan Doyle and Arabella. The thing they could not leave in the past.

As he talked about his work with the Society for Psychical Research, Beadle could see Conan Doyle give him the eye.

'I think Mr Doyle might have recognized you,' Arabella said.

'Perhaps it's you he recognizes.'

'No, he wouldn't remember me,' she said.

After a few minutes, Conan Doyle's face coloured and he avoided Beadle's penetrating gaze.

'There it is,' said Arabella. 'He's remembered.'

The lady in the back row turned again and shushed them.

The chairman invited questions from the audience and a lady near the front asked when the next Sherlock Holmes story was to be published. The chairman tried in vain to keep the talk to theosophy and quell all mention of the Baker Street detective, but it was not to be.

Arabella pulled on Beadle's arm and he took in her face again. She seemed suddenly sorrowful and lost. She pulled him away a little.

'I saw him,' she said. 'Tonight.'

'You did?'

'It could have been his son. In that you are right. But I felt it was him.'

'He looks so young?'

'Have you read *The Picture of Dorian Gray*, Inspector? It would explain so much. Do you think a good man can turn evil?'

He held her in his arms. It seemed appropriate right then, though it wasn't, not with him in his position, and she in hers.

'I've seen it too often, I'm afraid to say.'

'You're not really here on police business, though, are you, Inspector? This is a private thing. You are Captain Ahab, obsessed with the great white whale that escaped.'

She pulled away from him and he let his clumsy hands hang limp.

'The whale will pull you under,' she said.

'If you believe that, what are you doing here, with me?'

She stared into his eyes. This might be the moment to kiss her, he thought, if this were a love story. But they were not in a love story, they were in a murder mystery, and the detective did not kiss the victim in those sort of stories.

But what was in her eyes, he knew, was a torrent of understanding. That they were both being pulled under the sea by this need to put the past behind them.

A peal of laughter broke their gaze and Arabella Palmer looked at the floor, shook her head and stepped back to watch the performance. Beadle stood behind her, one arm around the cool, white pillar.

A journalist in the front row asked about Conan Doyle's involvement in the Edalji animal mutilations case in Great Wyrley.

'It is living proof,' said Conan Doyle, looking right at Beadle now, 'that the prime suspect is not always the culprit. It is not the first time I've had to investigate because the police pursued the wrong suspect.'

Beadle put his hand up and the chairman invited him to speak.

'Why is it that so many modern writers portray the police as bumbling incompetents, when the reality of policing in Britain is that your private detectives and amateur sleuths do not possess the special constabulary powers that would in fact be required to enable them to discharge the detective duties about which you write so freely?'

A gasp of outrage rippled through the audience, that someone dare criticize the greatest detective in the world.

Conan Doyle smiled and nodded. 'Perhaps we can trace it back to when public confidence in the police was broken forever by their failure to apprehend Jack the Ripper.'

They applauded, and one gentleman shouted, 'Hear, hear!'

'Do you think Sherlock Holmes could have caught him?' a lady asked.

'I'm sure he might,' said Conan Doyle. 'If only he'd been given the chance.'

The chairman drew the talk to a close and Conan Doyle signed copies of his new book.

Arabella stepped outside onto New Street and Beadle joined her under the gaslamp on the corner. New Street was desolate now. Life was elsewhere.

'I wonder,' he said, 'if our author friend ever got over his own disastrous attempt at amateur sleuthing. It would explain his increasingly hysterical portrayals of police incompetence.'

'Perhaps we are all making amends in our different ways,' she said.

Beadle sighed. 'You are right. This is personal for me. I have to make sense of it. But I fear an author of fantasies might make much more sense of it than I ever could.'

She nodded and smiled for the first time. '*There are more things in heaven and earth than are dreamed of in your philosophy.* Isn't that what Shakespeare tells us?'

'Through Hamlet, a character who is quite unhinged.'

'I think perhaps he is saner than any of us.'

Conan Doyle came rushing out, the lizard looking chairman manhandling him across the street to the station. It was his agent, that was obvious.

Stepping off the kerb, the author stopped and turned. 'Good evening. Inspector Beadle, if I remember rightly?' he said.

'Mister Conan Doyle. What a pleasure. I don't know that you ever got to meet Miss Arabella Palmer?'

Doyle gazed on her, trying to fit the face with the woman he had seen only fleetingly 24 years ago. 'Good Lord,' he said. 'I have no words. I can only offer my condolences.'

'We tend to offer condolences for the dead,' said Arabella.

'What if I told you,' said Beadle, 'that your old friend is back, and very much alive?'

Conan Doyle's eyes widened with shock. Then he smiled and nodded. 'I would say that would not surprise me. Sometimes the end of the story is also the beginning.'

He tipped his hat and the agent pulled him away across the street. They faded into the gaslit fog down the slope to the station entrance on Stephenson Street. It was clear that Arthur Conan Doyle knew nothing.

'I am to home,' said Arabella.

Beadle wondered if he should call in at the station. The thought made him despair. It had to be done, though. Pearce had been sighted yet again in Moseley and perhaps Joe Rees had something to report.

He pointed to the line of hansoms pulled up down the slope, forming a train behind Attwood's statue, which gazed down on the foot of Corporation Street.

'Come. I'll take you home,' Beadle said.

'No, no, I couldn't possibly.'

'Nonsense. I have to call at the station and time is of the essence, but I can see you safely home first.'

Beadle took Arabella's arm and walked her across the road to the cabstand. Down the slope of the hill, Conan Doyle and his agent disappeared into the mist. The horses stamped their feet and shook their manes against the cold.

He stepped up into the hansom cab and held out his hand, rather like Attwood's statue held out his hand – an eternal, forlorn question seeking an answer.

Arabella Palmer looked up and down New Street, then placed her hand in his and allowed him to pull her up to sit beside him.

— 31 —

The police station was a riot of swearing drunks being processed and photographed. A magnesium flash blinded Rachel for a moment and she heard Danny shout, 'You've got to let me go! She's in danger!'

The mob of police constables press-ganged the drunks before the photographer, each one holding up a chalkboard with their name and crime. They processed them swiftly, bullying the details out of them, while a constable scribbled the chalkboard, then shoved them in front of the camera before being frog-marched to the cells.

She had rushed into the reception area just in time to see Danny photographed. The board he held up said, *Daniel Pearce — No Fixed Abode — Drunkard.*

The grizzled sergeant held up a hand and growled, 'Who's in danger, sir?'

The constable stopped, holding Danny tight. This was Danny's last chance to convince them to let him go.

'Amy Parker,' he said. 'Her father's going to kill her on Saturday.'

The sergeant didn't seem surprised. 'And how do you know this?'

'I'm from the future.'

Rachel winced.

Everyone laughed but the sergeant. 'In you go,' he said.

The constable pushed Danny down the corridor where shouts and screams echoed off the walls.

Rachel walked up to the sergeant's desk. He was already writing out his report.

'Excuse me, sergeant,' she said. 'I'm with him. That last man. Daniel Pearce.'

He looked up and held her gaze with such authority that she lost her voice for a moment and just croaked.

'Oh yes?' he said. 'And are you from the future as well?'

'Er... No. I'm... Uh, sorry about him, sir. I'm afraid the gin was a bit too strong for him. He'll be normal in an hour.'

The sergeant looked her up and down. 'He may well be, madam,' he said. 'But he's staying in here for the night. You can stay too if you like?'

'No. That's fine, thank you. I'm sorry.'

She walked out as fast as she could, looking at her feet all the way until she was outside.

She stood there, stranded, wondering what to do. It was hopeless.

She set off walking up the dim street, hugging herself, not thinking about where she was going. She would have to go back home, to the present, and leave him here. Perhaps they would release him in the morning and he could make his own way back. Guilt gnawed at her. What if he somehow couldn't get back to the present? What if he were trapped here forever?

Staying here would be no help to him at all. It wouldn't change whether he could return home or not, and if the touchstone was going to change somehow and prevent them getting back, she would be trapped here too. She quickened her step and dug her hands in her pocket.

She felt the wad of family photographs in there.

A railway bridge over the road. She was taking the long route back to St Mary's. Her feet had decided to take her via Anderton Park Road. Her family's old house. She could see it as it was then. Her ancestors living there.

She marched through the dim back streets of lower Moseley and found the house. She took out the photograph of Mary Lewis, her great-great-grandmother, posing with a baby in her arms. A photograph that would be taken some time next year. She looked up from the photo to the former family home.

Nan was right. A house this big, back then, back now, meant they had money. Lots of money. She stared at the house for a while. The warm glow of light through the windows. The street was quiet and no one passed by.

They are in there now, she thought. The family that Nan remembers. She, Rachel, was the sole heir of this family. A genetic thread wound its way through a century, from Mary Lewis right to Rachel, and here she was, almost able to reach out and touch her.

She was about to carry on walking up the hill to head for St Mary's when someone emerged from a side entrance and walked towards her out of the gloom.

A young woman pulling on a jacket over her black maid's uniform. She slowed when she saw Rachel standing there and hovered uncertainly. Rachel stuffed the photos into her pocket.

'Hello,' said the girl. 'Are you calling on Mr Harper?'

It was Mary Lewis, quite clearly. But why was she in a maid's uniform?

'Er, no,' Rachel stammered. 'I was... I used to live in this house and I was just passing by and...'

'You used to live here?'

'Well, no. My family did.'

Mary wasn't sure what to do. She frowned with suspicion and Rachel recognized the same knitting of the brow from the photo.

'Ah,' said Mary Lewis.

'Harper, you say?'

'That's right. Mr and Mrs Harper. They've been here ten years.'

'Not Lewis?'

'Lewis? That's *my* name. I'm Mary Lewis.'

'You don't own this house then?'

'Me? Own it?' she said, almost laughing.

'But that doesn't… Did you have a baby this year?'

Mary looked horrified and her hand went to her belly. 'How do you… Look, who *are* you?'

Rachel now realized everything: her grandmother's delusions, her great-great-grandmother's lies. She backed away. 'I'm sorry,' she stammered. 'It's not this house at all. I'm in the wrong place.'

She marched off up the hill and broke into a run. Looking back as she ran, she saw Mary Lewis frozen with fear, staring after her, glancing back at the big house to see if anyone had witnessed it.

— 32 —

Arabella Palmer noticed that Inspector Beadle had kept hold of her hand. As the hansom cab rattled down the steep hill of Jamaica Row down to Digbeth, she felt herself lurching forward and was glad he held her firm.

He held her hand all the way along Digbeth High Street and she relaxed into the ride, enjoying the sensation as her flank bumped against his with each corner they took.

She was not used to carriages. They were an extravagance she could not justify. The tram had always suited her more, seeming more prudent, more democratic. It was something of a treat to be transported this way, a rare treat, and she wondered if he had hailed the cab in order to impress her. She hoped not. It was tiresome when a man thought he might take possession of a woman by paying for something, as if her head were on one of the coins in his pocket, like the king's.

He said nothing as they rode through Highgate. She turned to look at him as they passed the Balsall Heath public baths, the signs for Men and Women engraved in terracotta above the entrances. His eyes met hers and she thought he might say something, anything, but he held her gaze and did not shy away and she was thinking of so many things – that this man had seen her at the darkest moment of her life, that he'd been there to pull her from the depths of Hell, and how they had existed in the same square mile for all these years without speaking, only passing now and then in the street, and had he recognized her in all that time or was yesterday the first time?

She said nothing, only gazed into his eyes until a bump in the road made her look away.

And they were taking the gentle rise to Moseley now and would he still hold her hand as they crested the hill and rode down through the village, as brazen as you like? Would anyone see them riding like this and would they think he was courting her or perhaps had arrested her and was taking her to the station?

No, they sailed past Woodbridge Road, away from the station, so no one could think this was official police business, unless he was taking her home after interviewing her. What was it he called it? A person of interest. Was she a person of interest? Was that what people might say as they winked and nudged and laughed in that way they did about any man walking with any woman. Couldn't a woman talk to a man like she could talk to any woman and not have the world think she belonged to him? It was stupidity beyond belief that her sex prevented her from doing any of this – riding in this cab, holding this man's hand, being alone with him – without it meaning she had signed her life away to him, without it meaning that she was his property.

She was glad it was night and there was nothing but the occasional gaslight to show their faces. They went through the village, the battlements of St Mary's church tower pale against the black sky, and she wondered at Daniel Pearce and if he was there, watching her, seeing her with the policeman that had hounded him.

They passed the dovecote, standing alone and mysterious in the moonlight, and crested the final hill to ride down to Kings Heath high street.

She was glad that the driver veered left up Valentine Road

rather than take the busy high street. It was dark and quiet. She could almost hear her heart thumping above the clatter of the horse's hooves.

When they arrived on Woodville Road, the inspector did not wave her off and return to the police station as he had said he would. He stepped out with her. She let him murmur his words of farewell as he paid the driver. She opened the gate and went to her front door and felt him follow behind her. She said nothing.

Scrambling for the key, she opened the door swiftly and stepped inside to the dark hallway and he stepped in after her without a word. She thought he might have spoiled it by saying something or asking if he might come inside or invent some ridiculous excuse that would state in the open what they were doing, but he followed her in silence as if he understood what they both knew, and what this was. He closed the front door behind him with a resounding click that said this is happening, this is what it is.

For a moment they stood in blackness and she could hear his short, even breath, almost a sigh.

She switched on the electric light and looked at him again, a bold, brazen stare that challenged him to state his business. But he said nothing, simply gazed right back at her in that infuriatingly calm way he had about him. She wanted to slap the certainty right off his face. Who did he think he was, assuming anything about her? It was a gross impertinence.

'This is not the station,' she said.

'It would appear so,' he said,

As if he himself did not understand how he'd got here, as if he had woken from a hypnotist's trance to find himself standing on a cliff edge staring down into the deep sea and none of this was his own doing, his own decision. As if she had entranced him and brought him here to fall to his doom.

She felt no shame. She was a modern woman, an independent being with her own mind and will and heart.

She could have any guest she pleased in her own house at any time of day or night she chose.

She lunged for him, to slap him, sudden anger overwhelming her. But her hand met his cheek with barely the force of a kitten. It was more of a stroke than a slap, and in a moment, his lips were on hers.

And then it was all so clear. They were in this together as of now. Of course they were. Daniel Pearce had drawn them together. He was out there somewhere and they would find him together.

She sank into his embrace, and they plunged off the cliff to fall into the deep.

— 33 —

Rachel trudged back to St Mary's churchyard in a daze, hardly seeing anything around her. If she had stopped to think about it she might have wondered how she'd so quickly become immune to the newness of it all; walking through the village only a few hours earlier full of wonder at how different paving stones, street signs and lampposts were, and now walking ten minutes through gaslit streets as if she'd seen them all her life and didn't need to see them anymore.

She didn't notice the elegant townhouses along Wake Green Road, or that the mock Tudor row of dwellings along the upper part of St Mary's Row were still there, and she turned into the churchyard through the upper entrance, hardly noticing the railings that cordoned the path off from the jumble of gravestones, most of which were no longer there in her own time, or had become paving stones. She walked through almost pitch blackness down the path to the rear of the church and to the touchstone, absent-mindedly placing her palm to the correct spot, feeling the flush of heat and her ears pop as the industrial white noise of 2011 rushed into her head.

She found her carrier bag under the bush, fished her long coat out and took off her hat, leaving Danny's bag where it was.

She ambled home, slid her key into the lock and walked straight up the stairs, ignoring Olive walking out to greet her. Alone and safe in her room, she threw off her costume and put on jeans and a t-shirt and felt again a hundred years apart from that world she'd seen and breathed and lived, and at the same time not yet a part of this world where she'd always existed. She was stranded between two worlds, belonging to neither.

Later, she lay on her bed, flicking through the stack of old photos: Olive as a girl during the war posing with her parents outside the old house; Mary Lewis posing in front of the old house, not wearing her maid's uniform, a baby in her arms; and others, through the 1950s and 60s and 70s. Her ancestors. The timeline that defined her. All of it a huge lie.

They had not owned the big house. Mary Lewis had been a maid. They hadn't been rich. The family hadn't fallen on hard times. They'd always been this poor.

In the morning, she sat sullenly at the breakfast table, playing with her Sugar Puffs, watching Olive washing dishes, her dad rushing out of the door, a slice of jam on toast in his mouth, ruffling her hair as he breezed out, not noticing that her world had fallen apart.

She set off to the Central Library for a day of research, walking down the back streets of Moseley and scowling as she walked past the old house that had never belonged to her family.

— 34 —

'Inspector Beadle, you can wipe that smug smile off your face, right this minute.'

Arabella loosened her apron and pulled it off, which reminded him of last night. He smiled into his boiled egg as she joined him at the breakfast table.

'And I'd like to make it absolutely clear that I wait on you only as a guest, not because you are a man.'

'Oh, undoubtedly,' he said. 'Were this my house I would be serving breakfast to you.'

'As long as you know that.' She too had a smug smile on her face and crimson cheeks that matched the curtains.

They ate in silence, trying not to laugh out loud, and then she remembered something, leapt up and rushed upstairs. She came back down with an old leather-bound notebook and placed it on the pristine white tablecloth.

He sipped his tea and opened it to find vivid, violent swirls of colour. A sketchbook. An artist's sketchbook.

'You kept this?'

She nodded.

He remembered it from when it had been just another piece of evidence. Disturbing, violent scrawls, clearly the work of a madman. It had seemed so then, anyway. Less so now.

'There,' she said, prodding her finger at a page as he

flicked through. 'You see?'

A girl standing by a gravestone, a church behind her.

'It's St. Mary's, isn't it?'

'Yes. Absolutely.'

'He was obsessed with the place, and with that particular gravestone. He would take the shortcut through the graveyard and always stop at that gravestone, and could never say why it fascinated him so much. It's where I saw him again yesterday. That exact spot.'

Beadle wiped his face with a napkin, noting how civilized it made him feel – he did not bother with such affectations at home. Women had a way of making you your better self.

'This, then, is the key,' he said. 'Perhaps I could put a man there to wait for him to appear.'

'Could you do that?'

'No. I could not justify it.'

'I thought this was a private matter: our own private investigation?'

He pushed the book away and took her in. That mischievous smile at the corner of her defiant mouth. Those lips he had kissed for hours.

'Do you mean to make me an amateur detective? Like that ghastly Holmes creation?'

'Don't be mean. People like to believe in a gentleman sleuth with extraordinary powers of deduction.'

'Reality is much more mundane. I could tell you–'

'I believe you told Arthur Conan Doyle as much last night. You put him in his place.'

'I didn't do it to be mean.'

She rose and stood behind him, putting her arms around him and kissing his head. 'I know. I rather enjoyed you putting him in his place, Inspector Beadle.'

The echo of horses' hooves slowly clopping up the street, and the rattle of bottles.

'That's the milkman. You should go before the whole

world sees you leaving and there's a terrible scandal.'

'I do believe you would enjoy that too.'

He rose and put on his jacket and overcoat. She plonked his bowler on his head and pushed him to the door. He lingered at her lips, wanting to stay and melt into her again, but she shook her head and shooed him away, blushing.

He braced himself and stepped out into the morning fog.

In a moment, he was striding up the street, frost crackling underfoot, and no one had seen him leave.

He caught the tram to Moseley, feeling strangely alive, as if he had had a blood transfusion. All the blood coursing through his veins had been replaced with the blood of a younger man. He bounced into the station with an absurd grin on his face.

Sergeant Donaghy looked up from the front desk. 'Morning, sir. You're early.'

'Early bird catches the worm, Donaghy.'

'And the early worm gets eaten.'

'Quite so,' he chuckled.

'There's a message for you, sir.' Donaghy held up an envelope. 'Someone called last night, sir.'

He took it to his office. *Inspector Beadle – Urgent* scrawled on it.

Inside, a letter from Joe Rees.

Inspector Beadle,

I saw him again tonight. Our person of interest in the particular case of old. Namely, Mr D. Pearce! (or his son?)

He appeared again from the alley immediately opposite my place of work, no doubt having come through the churchyard of St. Mary's. Realising the importance of the moment, I locked up my cabin, with no thought to the financial cost to myself, and followed him.

The suspect was in the company of a young woman. The same as before. They walked along the Alcester Road northwards until they came to a house that was of particular interest to them (later confirmed as no. 12). The girl stood watch on the opposite side of the street, but DP went round to the rear of the premises.

In my surveillance, I circumnavigated the area and came to the rear of the row via the roads Trafalgar and Louise Lorne – whereupon I espied the suspect in conversation with a young lady at an upper story window – he having climbed onto the outhouse.

After a brief conversation, the suspect (DP) joined his accomplice at the front and they walked on northwards to Balsall Heath, and appeared to be in pursuit of the master of the house, one Mr Richard Parker.

I surmised this after calling at no. 12 and talking to the young lady of the house. She recognized me from my place of work but I think she did not suspect anything untoward.

Having earlier heard the suspects conversing as I passed, it is my considered opinion that they are plotting to murder Mr Parker with the assistance of his daughter.

I rushed to the station to report all to you but you had left.
Your servant, J.R.

Beadle shot up, his chair fell back, and he staggered free, the room swimming. Joe Rees was a fool. Good God, even the bloody newspaperman thought he could be a gentleman detective!

He read it again and again.

But it was good information. To hear them talk of murder and name Parker. That was good too. Joe Rees, the amateur bloody detective, had actually done rather well, even though he'd called at the door and named himself to a suspect.

Donaghy knocked and entered with a pile of slim manila folders. 'The overnights, sir.'

Beadle took them.

Donaghy's eyes flitted to the chair and the letter in

Beadle's hand. 'Everything all right, sir?'

A private investigation, Arabella had said. Not official business at all. He couldn't make it official, despite what was in Joe's letter. Not just yet. There were too many strange factors to this case that made his neck cringe.

'Everything's fine, Donaghy. Thank you.'

The overnights. Official police business. He would go through them and do his dogged duty and perhaps then visit the Parker household.

Righting his chair, he sat and went through the arrest reports, noting the increase of incidents on the previous night. His eyes marked the calendar. Friday the 24th November. Full moon tomorrow.

Donaghy came again with a cup of tea. It wasn't so bad first thing in the morning. It was later when the urn produced a foul sludge.

His eyes.

A gunshot snatched the sound from his ears. His breath. His hold on the world.

His eyes, staring from the mugshot. It was him. Holding up a chalk board with a few numbers and the words *Daniel Pearce — No Fixed Abode — Drunkard* in Sergeant Donaghy's scrawl.

Here. In this station.

The teacup fell and exploded.

He ran out, down the corridor, to the cells. Empty. Rising panic in his heart.

He darted to the front desk and slammed the arrest report before Donaghy. 'This man! Where is he?'

'What? Him?'

'Yes! Him!'

'He's gone, sir. Only ten minutes ago. You must have passed him as you came in.'

'Dear God, why did you let him go?'

Donaghy shrank back, stammered, wondering what he'd

done that was so bad. 'He was a drunk, sir. We keep them in till they're sober and kick them out first thing.'

He wasn't to know. He knew nothing of Pearce and murder and the Parker family. How could he?

'He was rambling and intoxicated when arrested. Said he was from the future. But he was perfectly sober this morning.'

That roaring in his ears again, like a ghost was trying to contact him from the beyond. Or just the sea. The great white whale escaping.

He rushed out to the street and looked up and down, knowing he would be nowhere in sight. He was long gone. But he knew where.

He ran back to his office. Tea all over the floor. The arrest report still in his hand. He folded it and shoved it in his overcoat pocket. Put on his hat and coat and marched out.

Pausing on the station steps, he thought of Arabella. He should call her. It was her business too. But there was no time. He knew exactly where Pearce would be and if he rushed, he would have him.

— 35 —

Danny, curled up on a wooden bench in a crowded cell, realized what the phrase *chilled to the bone* meant: he felt it deep in his marrow through the night and shook so uncontrollably he couldn't sleep.

In the morning, the huge, whiskered police sergeant unlocked the cell and discharged them all with a warning. He found himself outside, blinking at the morning fog, stretching himself, every joint aching.

He was surprised to find the streets already crowded with horse-drawn cabs, electric trams full of people heading for the city, barrow boys wheeling carts of merchandise to the shops.

Walking down Alcester Road would be too crowded, he thought. He would be too exposed. Something told him to keep to the shadows. He walked up Woodbridge Road, past the Trafalgar pub and turned into Trafalgar Road. Tramping down the hill till he came to Louise Lorne Road on his left – a narrow lane between houses.

He was coming to it from the opposite side he had last night. The lane gave out to the tree-lined square behind Amy Parker's house. He could see her window.

He vaulted the fence again and crouched in the back garden out of sight of neighbouring houses. Throwing stones at her window. There was no answer. Perhaps they were out.

He sprinted to the outhouse and edged around it to the side yard. A window looked out onto the yard – the middle room that was perhaps a drawing room or dining room – but there was no sign of life.

His back to the wall, he skirted the yard and peered inside the kitchen. A girl at the kitchen sink. Was it the maid? She turned and her eyes met his.

A yelp of surprise. Her hand to her mouth.

It was Amy.

Glancing back into the house, she darted for the back door. He met her there and lunged for her lips. She shrank back, fear in her eyes and he realized it was too much, too soon. He had talked to her only twice.

'What are you doing here?' she hissed.

He stepped inside and she let him close the back door, glancing again into the house.

'I had to see you again,' he said. 'To warn you.'

'Father's in bed with a migraine. Please don't wake him.'

'We don't need to wake him,' he whispered. 'In fact, it's perfect.'

'It's far from perfect. He has them all the time. He can't get up, can't go to his office. I'm about to telephone to let them know. It's his business. He employs three clerks.'

She was rambling, confused, as if the thread holding her life together was unravelling.

'Listen to me, Amy.'

'The maid has walked out too. Says she can't cope with father's strange moods.'

'This is good, too.'

'It's not. It all falls down to me to save us. We are close to shipwreck.'

She knotted her fingers and couldn't look at him, distracted, distraught. He took her hands in his.

'Listen, Amy. There's something I have to tell you. About your father.'

She looked up into his eyes, just as she had the first moment he'd seen her, entreating him to tell her, even though she already knew. 'What is it?'

'You need to come with me,' he said.

'I can't. Not today.'

'You *have* to, before tomorrow.'

His intensity stilled her. He was sure she could read it in him: that she was in great danger from the man upstairs, the man she both feared and wanted to protect.

'Why before tomorrow?'

'Just come with me,' he said. 'Let's get away from here.'

'I can't,' she whispered.

'Amy, you're not safe.'

'What is it?' she said. 'What's going to happen?'

He held her, his hands stroking her arms, wanting to kiss her, wanting to run with her.

'You know it, don't you? You know I'm here to help you.'

'I don't even know you.'

'You know it feels right, though. To come with me, right now.'

She stared into his eyes. She seemed to know it.

'I'm taking you away from here,' he said, suddenly forceful and praying she would give in to him. 'Now. You understand?'

'Where are we going?'

'I'm going to take you somewhere safe. Somewhere he won't find you.'

'Where?'

'You wouldn't believe me if I told you,' he said. 'Let's go. Now.'

She stared, stricken, paralysed. He would have to drag her out of there, drag her all the way to the present.

The doorbell rang. A harsh buzz.

Amy broke free from him.

'Don't answer it.'

'I have to. It will wake father. Wait here and hide till they're gone. But if it's the maid, you have to run away. Perhaps she's changed her mind and needs the money. Yes, that might be it.'

She walked out of the kitchen, through the middle room and down the long hallway to the front door. The bell rang again.

Danny skipped across the dining room, closing the door to the hall so he could peep through the crack.

Amy opened the door. It was an old man in a bowler hat and greatcoat.

'Miss Parker, I believe,' he said.

'And who might you be?' she asked.

'Inspector Beadle,' he said. 'I wish to talk with you about a Mr Daniel Pearce. I believe you've met him recently?'

The inspector stepped inside and Amy retreated.

'I don't know who you mean, Inspector,' she said, turning and looking right at Danny.

The inspector too peered over her head, right at the crack in the door. 'Is he here now?'

Danny stepped back, creeping across the dining room rug. He hurtled through the kitchen and out of the back door just as the inspector's voice came through the dining room.

'Only he's been sighted here and he's a person of interest in…'

He was out and sprinting up the back garden, hidden by the outhouses. He took a running leap at the fence and was over it, crashing to the ground on the other side, a searing shot of pain through his knee.

He limped up the quiet lane of Louise Lorne Road, casting glances behind him. No police in pursuit. As he ran on, he wondered how the police had come to be involved, and how the hell did they know his name?

There was nothing for it. He had to go back and plan this. There was still time to get her away from her father, even if it had to be tomorrow.

He limped onto Trafalgar Road and was about to climb the hill when he paused. No, he wouldn't go home just yet. There was something else he needed to do first.

He turned left and headed for Highgate.

— 36 —

Amy Parker tried to slow her pace as she walked up the hall, but the inspector brushed her to the side and pushed through. He knew she was lying.

He burst into the dining room, expecting to see Danny Pearce, but there was nothing. He must have run out the back.

'Really, what is the meaning of this, Inspector?' she protested.

He bowled through the kitchen. The back door was open. She followed him out to the garden and found it was totally quiet and empty.

The inspector peeped behind the outhouses, and even looked in the privy, but there was no sign that Danny Pearce had ever been here.

'Are you quite satisfied?' she demanded.

'Was he here?'

'I don't know who you mean, I'm sure!'

He looked her up and down, sizing her up.

She held his cold gaze and saw that her cocksureness disarmed him. But he knew she was hiding something.

He followed her back into the house, through the kitchen. Someone tramping on the stairs. Had Danny hidden behind the door and waited for the inspector to run through to the garden, having left the back door open as bait?

'What is this!' a voice roared.

Oh, God.

'Father,' she stammered. 'This is a police inspector.'

'Inspector Beadle,' he said quickly, as if he also sensed that his innocence needed to be ascertained immediately in case Father murdered him. Beadle producing his identity papers.

This wiped the anger from Father's face and he switched, in a flash, to the concerned demeanour of an upstanding pillar of society.

'Inspector? How can I help? Is this about Rieper? Poor chap. We buried him Wednesday.'

Here it was again. Father always acted normal when the right people called. His madness dissipated. This was a good thing.

The inspector looked from Amy to her father. 'Indeed,' he said. 'Just following up on a few things. Routine, you understand.'

'You must forgive my state,' father said. 'I am rather ill with a recurring migraine. Hence you find me at home.'

'I do apologize. I should come back at a more convenient time.'

'When the lodge is open at three degrees both within and without,' said father.

'I'm sorry?'

'Numbers fourteen eighteen,' father said, smiling.

The inspector stared, trying to make sense of it.

Amy put on a smile. 'Father, your migraine has made you disoriented. You should go back to bed.'

'Numbers fourteen eighteen. She knows that.'

The inspector was thrown. Would he take Father away?

Instead, Beadle tipped his hat and said, 'I must go.'

'Fourteen eighteen,' father cackled.

Amy pushed the inspector out of the dining room and down the hall. He was happy to go now, as if he had stepped into something that was altogether too strange for him. He was a plodding policeman, quite dull and boring, nothing like the detectives one read about in books and magazines.

'Numbers fourteen eighteen!' Father called from behind, thankfully rooted to the spot, not following. He was an anarchist's bomb about to explode and only she knew it.

She opened the door and almost shoved the inspector outside. She didn't care if he fell flat on his face, as long as he saw no more of her father's madness.

But the inspector wheeled round and stood firm. 'I know he was here,' he said. He pulled out a photograph and shoved it in her face.

Daniel Pearce, arrested, like a common criminal. She snatched the photograph and peered closer. There was no mistaking it was him.

'When was this?'

'Last night.'

'That can't be so. He was here last night and he was not drunk.'

'So you know him.'

She shook her head. 'I only saw him two days ago, at Mr Rieper's funeral. He calls himself Danny, not Daniel.'

The inspector snatched the photograph back. 'I must warn you, Miss Parker, that this man was once a suspect in a murder enquiry.'

'Murder?'

'You are in grave danger. Do not answer the door to him again. If he calls, telephone me on this number.'

He gave her a calling card.

'He's not a murderer,' she said. 'That can't be.'

'There was a murder. He was a person of interest.'

'How long ago?'

The inspector shifted uncomfortably and looked up and down the street. A tram sailed past.

'That doesn't matter.'

He cast one more glance over her shoulder at the madness behind her, then turned away. She closed the door and fell back against it, her tears falling on his name.

Inspector Beadle.

Danny Pearce had come to protect her, though. That's what he had said. To protect her from her father.

And she was caught in the middle, protecting her father. This house was the Titanic and she alone knew of the iceberg lying wait in the dark waters ahead. If they put him in the asylum, she would be better off dead. Everything would be gone. Shipwrecked.

Sundered.

The inspector had been too concerned with Danny Pearce to see The Secret – the shameful secret – in this house. She had to guard that secret, protect father, save him from the same fate as his mad mother.

She alone could prevent the sinking of the Titanic, so they might harbour safely in New York and celebrate.

— 37 —

Highgate didn't feel as dangerous in daylight. There were no gangs of drunks hanging around outside pubs seething with violence, and the morning mist was not as menacing as the night fog.

Danny strode up to the pharmacy and looked through the window with its display of bottles of blue and red liquid. There was no one but the elderly pharmacist and his assistant. He pushed the door and stepped inside, the bell announcing his arrival.

They looked up. The assistant recognized him.

'Hello again, sir,' he said.

Danny was thrown. No one ever called him 'sir' and it felt strange, like being called 'm'lord' or 'your honour'.

'Good morning,' he said, stepping forward and addressing the older man. 'I'd like to speak with you, if I may.'

The assistant flushed red. His boss frowned.

'Certainly, sir,' said the old man.

'It's, er, a delicate matter. Could I speak with you privately?'

He glanced at the door with its brass notice marked *Private*.

'Of course. Follow me, sir.'

The assistant suddenly stammered. 'I hope nothing

untoward has happened with your lady friend?'

Danny could see he was panicking, thinking the worst. 'No, no, no,' he said. 'She's absolutely fine. You made her much better. This is a totally different matter.'

The assistant heaved a sigh of relief and bowed his head.

The old man frowned again and walked to the door, holding it open for Danny to follow. They climbed a set of steep wooden stairs and walked into a small oak-panelled room with a mahogany desk. The pharmacist took a seat at the desk and indicated the free chair.

'Now, sir, how may I help you?'

'I... don't know how to say this...'

'Be assured, sir, you can divulge anything here. We are utterly discreet.'

Danny could hear the traces of another accent through his attempt at formal English. Was he foreign? He noticed the slight fray of his cuffs and remembered how worn down his heels had been as he'd followed him up the stairs.

'There was a man here, last night,' he said, trying on the official tone of a police inspector. 'A Mr Parker. I'd like to ask you some questions about him.'

The pharmacist glared with sudden fear. 'Is this a police matter?' he croaked.

'Not exactly. More a private investigation.'

The pharmacist's lips pursed and he rose from his seat. 'I'm afraid I can't help you, sir. I deal with my... patients... in the strictest confidence. I have to ask you to leave now.'

Danny felt his resolve fading. He reached into his inside pocket and pulled out a sheaf of notes. The pharmacist looked confused for a moment, then much less confused as Danny laid one of the notes on the desk.

'I'm afraid I really must insist that you...'

Danny laid another note on top of the first and the pharmacist wheezed a little.

'Please, sir,' he stammered.

Danny put a third note down and shoved the rest back in his pocket. The pharmacist had actually begun to sweat, pearls of perspiration dotting his bulging neck. He glanced around, as if someone in the room might witness him about to commit a crime. He gazed at the money for a long time, like it was singing to him. Danny watched, curious as to the mesmeric effect these absurdly large, crispy sheets of paper had on him. The pharmacist blinked himself out of his trance, looked at Danny's blank face, swallowed, nodded slightly and, as if being sent to fetch the cane that would be used on him, hobbled across the room and took a wooden box off the shelf.

When he brought it back to the table, Danny could see that it wasn't a box but a case with a leather strap for a handle. The pharmacist nodded to him, urging him to open it. Danny flipped the box open and found that the case was divided inside into several sections, each containing a selection of tools. There was a long glass cylinder that ran the length of the case and appeared to collect at one end into a rubber teat from which ran a rubber tube that was coiled all the way and collected inside the cylinder in the opposite, open end. Measurements were engraved into the side of the glass, starting at 50 and running up to 300. A circular compartment held a porcelain dish, locked in place with moveable brass pegs. There was an enamel container the size of a cigarette holder, and a few bottles. One of them was a dropper and two contained liquid, labelled *Hydrochloric Acid* and *Salvarsan*.

Danny looked up at the pharmacist, whose face seemed to say that he'd divulged some great secret. Danny shrugged. 'What is this?'

The pharmacist frowned and slammed the case shut with sudden annoyance.

'I've shown you everything,' he said. 'I shall not write it down for you also. Now. Please. Go.'

Danny rose and walked to the door, not sure what he'd just seen. He looked back and was surprised to see the pharmacist slumped in the chair, one hand covering his eyes, the other scraping the notes towards him.

— 38 —

Rachel buried herself in the Local Studies section for the day. She had always liked to do this: disappear into archives, following leads, methodically building up a picture of the past, not realising where she'd been for hours or that she'd missed lunch and was ravenous. What she found in the Central Library that morning should have shocked her, but she was trapped in a cloud of numbness and stared at it with a sense of inevitability, almost as if she'd expected to find it there.

Flipping through a modern photo book titled *Birmingham's Victorian & Edwardian Criminal Underground*, each page a series of mugshots from police archives, she found herself staring at Danny's face in washed out black-and-white, holding up a chalk board with a few numbers and the words *Daniel Pearce — No Fixed Abode — Drunkard*.

Just as he had last night.

This was the instant the photographer's camera had flashed and blinded her, the magnesium flare still floating in her vision even when she had stood staring at the old family house. This was the moment Danny had been arrested, a photograph that had sat in the archives for a hundred years, recorded here in this book ten years ago. It had been here, hidden in the pages of this book even two days ago when they'd first come here, before they'd hired the costumes and gone back to 1912.

She went to the photocopier by the Information desk and pushed in coins to take a copy of it. The redheaded librarian eyed her curiously, and Rachel wondered if she was going to be told off for copying protected material.

'You're doing the project with your student friend, aren't you?' she said.

'Yes, that's right.'

'Is he not in today?'

'No, he's been held up. Somewhere else.'

The librarian handed her a photograph in a cellophane bag. 'He asked me to search for this. I found it in the archive we have of a local portrait photographer. We don't always have the names, but this photographer was fairly meticulous in cataloguing his subjects, so I managed to find it.'

Rachel slipped the photograph out of the cellophane wrapper and found herself looking at Richard Parker, a respectable Edwardian businessman, standing erect, one thumb tucked into his waistcoat pocket, a hand on the shoulder of his daughter, Amy, seated on a stool, hands on her lap, both grim faced, a fake drawing room backdrop behind them.

'Thank you,' Rachel said. 'I'll give it to him.'

The librarian watched her go back to her desk, her polite smile fading.

Rachel studied all afternoon and was about to leave when something occurred to her. She walked over to the Directories stack and ran her fingertip along the row of red and black Kelly's Directories till it rested on the 1912 edition. She slid it out and opened it, smelling its musty pages, but instead of flipping to Alcester Road, she found Anderton Park Road, her finger sliding down to number 28, and the head of household.

Mr Reginald M. Harper.

She closed the book and frowned.

Her phone vibrated in her pocket. She took it out and read the text message from Danny.
I'm back.

— 39 —

Arabella Palmer's heart leapt as she opened the door to Beadle. She turned and let him follow her inside and waited till he shut the front door before she fell on him, kissing him so deeply right there in the hallway, unable to wait a moment longer.

They kissed for what felt like an hour, and she moaned against him, wanting him so utterly with a naked need she hadn't known she could feel again in her life.

Then he had to spoil it all by telling her about his day.

She sat in the parlour and listened as he paced the Persian rug and told her about the letter from his informant, and the arrest report that revealed Daniel Pearce had been in the police cells all night.

'He was there. Right there in my own cell, and I missed him, by mere moments,' he said.

She didn't like the inference that he'd missed him because he'd been here, with her.

Then she listened with growing fury as he relayed the investigation at the Parker household.

'I must say, I had an eerie thought. The similarity in your names. Twenty-four years ago this man was about to marry you, *Arabella Palmer*. Now he, or his son, is drawn to *Amy Parker*. Could there be something in the names? Is this a clue, a key to unlock this mystery?'

'Yes, perhaps it was my initials all along.'

He didn't see. He didn't notice her anger, the dolt. He kept on blathering about the strange meeting with Richard Parker.

'There was something off about him. I thought the daughter was protecting him, protecting some secret. He appeared perfectly lucid and normal, but then he answered as if he were addressing someone else altogether, in a separate conversation, perhaps from the past.'

'I don't know what you mean.'

'He kept repeating something odd. *Numbers fourteen eighteen,* he said. And this was what his daughter knew. *Numbers fourteen eighteen.* Is that a year? What happened in 1418? Do you have an historical almanac?'

'There's nothing I can think of,' Arabella said. 'But if it was a date he would just say *1418*, why say they are numbers? Perhaps it's a mathematical problem.'

'Yes, you're right.'

'You needn't sound surprised at that.'

He looked up from his reverie and finally noticed. 'Arabella, you are angry with me.'

'Why would I be angry with you?'

'I have no idea.'

She folded her arms. He really was perfectly obtuse, and no different to the majority of men.

He slapped his forehead. 'You resent that I went alone, without you.'

'It was to be *our* investigation,' she said.

'Arabella. I'm a Detective Inspector. What am I to do when a suspect is brought to my attention and is only minutes away?'

'You said it was not official business. It was a private matter. You said we shared it.'

He flapped his arms hopelessly and let them fall to his

side. 'You are right. I apologize. I did think of you, but I knew it would waste time and he might be gone. And I didn't feel I could call on them pretending it was official police business if I had my... *You* with me.'

'Your what?'

'*You,* I said.'

'You were going to say *with your...* What *am* I?'

'My fiancé,' he mumbled, like it was stupid, like it was embarrassing to him. He looked at the rug.

'I don't recall a proposal.'

He went down on one knee, so suddenly he grunted with the effort. 'Arabella Palmer, would you do me the honour of being my wife?'

She recoiled. It was rather sweet and impulsive and her heart fluttered, even though it was not the proposal she had ever imagined.

'I'll think about it,' she said.

'Oh.'

'I have some conditions.'

'Name them.'

He took her fidgeting hands in his own.

'We have a year-long engagement. I want to see what kind of man you are before I commit to the rest of my life.'

'That can happen,' he said.

'My membership of the suffragette movement continues and is non-negotiable. Even if I am imprisoned.'

'Done.'

'Even if you have to arrest me yourself.'

'Good God, Arabella–'

'That is also non-negotiable.'

He thought about it, and she could see the cogs whirring in his mind: how he was retiring soon anyway, weighing up the chance to marry her against a few more years shuffling papers in Moseley police station.

'I agree,' he said.

'And if we are to be married, I will not promise to obey you. But I will love and honour you, if you will do the same for me.'

'That is rather radical,' he said. 'I don't know that we'll get a vicar to agree to that.'

'Of course,' she cried. 'That's it!' She snapped her fingers and rushed to the bookshelf.

He got up from his knee and sat with a sigh. He really was in no fit state to be chasing criminals.

She heaved a thick volume down and slammed it on her lap, sitting next to him.

'The Bible? Do you want me to swear on it?'

'Not that, silly.'

She flicked through the thin scritta pages, through *Judges, Joshua* and *Deuteronomy*, till she came to it.

'The Book of Numbers,' he said. 'Of course.'

She flipped to Chapter 14, her finger gliding down the page to verse 18. *'The Lord is patient and full of mercy, taking away iniquity and wickedness, and leaving no man clear, who visitest the sins of the fathers upon the children unto the third and fourth generation.'*

'Numbers fourteen eighteen,' he said. 'You think this is what he meant?'

'He said his daughter knew it, didn't he?'

'He's going to punish her for his sins?'

'Or he thinks God is going to do that. He's a rather cruel God to do that, don't you think?'

Beadle stood and paced again. 'Tomorrow we should go to St. Mary's. That is key to this mystery. And while we're there, we can talk with Reverend Colmore.'

'Is this about our wedding arrangements?' She smiled, so he would know she was teasing him.

'Not just yet,' he said. 'You want a long engagement, remember?'

— 40 —

Rachel texted Danny that she was in the library. In an hour, he came, still in his Edwardian suit, although with his shirt collar open he simply looked like a retro hipster, nothing too unusual. He had his carrier bag, which must have contained his hat. It was funny how in films people looked at a time traveller and noticed how strangely they were dressed. In reality, no one noticed much at all. It was another thing the movies had all wrong.

He slid into the chair beside her and threw his head back. 'You won't believe what's happened.'

'How was prison?'

'Grim as. I'm just glad that drunk wasn't in there with me. I'm going to get Amy to run away with me. If she runs away with me, it can't happen. Which means she can't die.'

Rachel glanced around. There were a handful of people in the Local Studies section, but all too far away to hear. The redheaded librarian girl was watching them from her reception desk, but she couldn't hear them.

'Do you think it's healthy falling in love with a girl who's over a hundred?'

'I like mature women,' he laughed, spinning the revolving chair.

He was in love with himself more than Amy Parker, that

was clear. It was all about Danny Pearce and how brilliant he was to cheat time. It had always been about him and his control, never about the past and what it meant just to see it, observe it, maybe even learn from it. It was a giant river and you could sit on the banks and watch it. But Danny wanted to drive a digger into it and alter its course, just so he could say *I did that.*

'I found out what *General Paralysis* means,' she said.

'I know what it means.'

'What do you mean? You thought it meant just *dead*, you said.'

'I know. And then I found out what it really meant,' he smiled, holding up his smartphone.

He was so infuriatingly smug she wanted to slap him.

'It's the polite term for syphilis,' she said, realising she was blurting it out before he could. 'They put it on death certificates so it wouldn't cause a scandal. That's why he's mad. It eats away at the spinal cord or something. Sends you crazy.'

'I know,' he smiled. 'He goes to that chemist in Highgate for Salvarsan injections. It's a revolutionary new treatment. In 1912. But I think it's come a little too late for Mr Parker. It's certainly come too late for Amy.'

'You can't save her, Danny,' she said.

'Just watch me.'

'It's already happened.'

'Not yet it hasn't.'

She reached for the stack of books in front of her and pulled out the photo book, holding it up in front of him.

'Look at this.'

She flipped through pages of mugshots till she came to his picture.

'There.'

He took it from her, staring in wonder.

'Daniel Pearce,' she said. 'No Fixed Abode. Drunkard.

Arrested a hundred years ago.'

'So that's how he knew my name,' he said.

'What do you mean?'

'An inspector called on Amy, this morning. I was there. He asked her about me. I had to run out the back door.'

'The police are looking for you? They know you're up to something with Amy? Jesus, Danny, you have to stop.'

'Edwardian cops are so slow. I don't think they'd ever catch me.'

'They caught you yesterday. You want to go back to an Edwardian prison that much?'

He just stared at his photo in the book with a stupid grin. 'This is awesome. I need to get a copy of this.'

He was such an idiot. 'Don't you get it?'

'What?'

'This book has been in this library for years. Your photo's been in it for years. Before you got arrested yesterday, before you met Amy Parker, maybe even before you were born.'

'Mad, isn't it?'

'Yes, it is! It's mad that you think you can change anything. She's dead. It's in the archives right here. It's already happened. Just like your arrest.'

He shook his head. 'Well, I'm going to change it.'

He looked over his shoulder and checked the librarian. She was watching, but at his look she turned and busied herself shifting stock. Danny ripped the page out of the book, folded the page and tucked it inside his pocket.

He winked.

She wanted to vomit in his face. 'You're used to getting what you want, aren't you?'

'I don't know what that means.'

'It's just a playground to you. Just a game. It's all laid on for your personal amusement and you're going to change the past just because you *can!*'

'What are you talking about?'

'Have you ever thought there might be some things you can't change? Have you ever thought maybe some things are just never going to change?'

Tears pricked her eyes and she turned so he wouldn't see. He couldn't see anything but his own desire, anyway.

'No. I haven't,' he said. 'That's why I'm not like you.'

She snatched up her bag and stood. 'Just leave her alone, Danny.'

She marched off, across acres of orange carpet, and stomped down the escalators.

Outside it was night and a fierce wind blew through Chamberlain Square. She shuddered, hugging her thin jacket closer, her belly rumbling, longing for the safety of home and Nan's overcooked dinner. Home seemed a million miles away.

Trudging through the city, she decided that in the morning she would have to find a way to stop Danny changing history. She didn't know why she needed to – it meant nothing to her – but somehow it seemed like it was a matter of life or death not for Amy Parker, but for Rachel too.

— 41 —

Danny worked on alone on the sixth floor, which slowly thinned as people packed up their research and went home. He noticed it was mostly old men, retired, working through archives, trying to find their past, living out their final days in a world they could never have.

He was different. He could live in that past, a past they could never grasp. He laughed as he imagined striking up conversation with one of them to find out a little about their research, to find out where they longed to be again, so he could go to that time and screw it up for them. Just for the fun of it.

He didn't have a pen or paper on him, only his phone, which was running low on battery. He was unprepared for this, he thought, then laughed at his ability to visit the past, be in it, change it.

He walked over to the reception desk and noticed the exhibition on the Titanic. The 100-year anniversary. Photocopied pages of the ship, its captain, the newspaper report about the terrible loss of life. Amy had read that actual newspaper, and it was *news* to her. And he, could he go back and change it? Go back to a little earlier and warn them of the iceberg, warn everyone that the ship was going to sink? Could he somehow control *when* the touchstone would let him go to? So that if he failed to save Amy tomorrow, he could try again and again till he got it right?

The redheaded librarian on reception desk seemed startled to see him.

'Hi,' he said. 'I've been very silly and come out without a pen and paper. Would you be able..?'

She smirked. 'Doesn't your girlfriend have one?'

'What? Oh, Rachel. She's not... No. She's gone.'

Was she checking him out? How could he tell her that he was only interested in a girl from 100 years ago; how could she possibly even begin to understand that?

She slid a couple of sheets of A4 scrap paper across the desk and an old biro.

'There's something I need to find out. I wonder if you can help?' he said.

'That's what I'm here for.'

'There's a murder that happens in 1912 and I'm trying to find out the exact time of day it happened. I've looked for newspaper reports but there's nothing, do you have police reports?'

She shook her head and ran her hand through her hair, even though it was pinned back in a bun. 'We don't have anything like that.'

'What about asylum records? I know the killer was committed to Winston Green asylum.'

'Ooh, we do have those records, actually. Do you have a name?'

He wrote it down, Richard Parker's name and age, the date of Amy's death – tomorrow, exactly 100 years ago – and ripped off a square of paper for her.

'Let me check,' she said.

She walked off and took a spiral staircase to an upper archive room. He couldn't help examining her legs as she climbed the stairs. Back in 1912 that would be shocking, seeing that much of a woman, almost pornographic, and here it was nothing. He realized he hadn't seen so much as Amy Parker's bare elbow.

He sat back at his desk and a gnawing pain in his gut reminded him he hadn't eaten all day. A sudden blanket of fatigue weighed on him.

'You're lucky.'

He opened his eyes. The redheaded librarian was standing over him with a large, square cardboard box. She placed it on his desk.

'I should make you come back tomorrow as there's a privacy law that covers this for exactly 100 years. But I'll let you off.'

'Lucky me,' he said.

'Sign this.'

She gave him a chit to sign to say he had them and he wouldn't take photographs or steal them or release the information into the public domain ahead of the hundred-year privacy rule.

He opened the box and found various old folders full of reception reports and statements. Flicking through the names he thought Parker would be missing but it was the last in the box.

The pages were musty and mottled with damp. The whole Local Studies section smelt of this. Most of the library, in fact. The past reeked of it. But it wasn't the past at all. The past didn't smell like that. It was all the time between then and now that had that disgusting smell.

The reception report was brief. Someone had scribbled answers to a series of printed entries. He read the entire thing, the whole sad history of Richard Parker arriving disoriented, talking in riddles about 'closing the lodge at three degrees both within and without' and answering almost every question put to him with the response, 'numbers fourteen eighteen', till he deteriorated rapidly and died after a fit.

A fit. That was it. You could have a fit and just die.

There was nothing about the time of the attack, so he combed through it again. There must be something there to tell him when he'd arrived, if only that.

Then he found it.

In tiny writing, amid a section where most of the entries had been left blank.

Reason for admittance: Violent fits. Murdered daughter. 11.44 am.

And later. *Time of admittance: 3.10 pm.*

11.44.

He had it now. The exact time of the attack on Amy. He thought wildly, trying to calculate back from that point. Was that the time of her death, or the time of his arrest? Might he have killed her earlier than that and only been arrested at 11.44?

He checked his phone. Now displaying Amy Parker's face as his screensaver. It was nearly 8pm. She would be dead in exactly fifteen hours and forty-four minutes' time.

If he got there early in the morning, he would stop it. Ten o'clock would be enough. But this wasn't some lecture he could turn up late for. He had to get this right.

11.44.

He was the only person in the world who knew this was going to happen, at that exact time. And that meant he was the only person in the world who could stop it.

He could make sure it never happened.

He packed the papers back in the box and took them to reception.

'I was just about to chuck you out,' the librarian said. 'We're closing now.'

He hadn't heard the reminders over the tannoy. It was eight. He had to go home and sleep and be up early in the morning.

He had an important date with history.

— 42 —

Inspector Beadle woke with a terrible hangover and remembered with annoyance that he hadn't drunk anything last night. A strange dissociated feeling, like he wasn't in his own body, a throbbing, nagging pain at the back of his head, and a keen thirst.

The full moon. It always made him feel like this. A dread of the impending criminal upheaval.

He had proposed.

Arabella Palmer had accepted his offer of marriage. He grinned as he washed and dressed, looking around his Spartan bachelor house. Would she come to live here or would he go to hers? He touched the lips of his wife in the photograph above the mantelpiece, as he did every morning, but this time lingered longer.

'I'm to marry again, Hermione,' he said. 'I know you said I should, but I didn't think I ever would. She's a good lady. I'm not sure you would approve of her political beliefs, but I know you'd like her as a woman. As do I.'

He remembered their son, James, and looked at his feet. And I must re-connect with him too, he thought. Tell him this news. I do hope he will cease blaming me for your death, Hermione. Perhaps the angry young man had mellowed and wouldn't resent his father re-marrying.

He straightened his tie, as Hermione used to, and as Arabella soon would, and stepped out into the fog and frost of the morning, pulling his muffler tighter around his neck.

He had thought it appropriate to leave Arabella, not stay the night as he already had. The promise of marriage had invoked a sense of chasteness, but he wondered if they might last a year without giving in to that urgent, primal need for each other.

He caught the tram to the police station and put in a morning shift, to avoid the sense of guilt that he would slope off for his eleven o'clock appointment with Arabella at St Mary's. A private investigation. Even so, he watched the clock until it turned to 11.00.

— 43 —

Rachel woke and her eyes fell on her bedside clock. The first few moments of uncertainty as she slipped between two worlds.

She had dreamt that her house was locked and she couldn't find a way inside. She was banging on the windows, Dad and Nan inside watching the telly, not hearing her, even though she screamed.

It was Saturday morning. 10.30.

She knew what she had to do. She got up and showered and ignored the Edwardian dress splayed across her bedroom floor. She put on her maxi skirt, DMs and the velvet Goth jacket she'd bought from Oasis. Since visiting the past, she had felt awkward dressing in anything too revealing.

Martyn and Olive were pottering about in the kitchen and the sweet smell of bacon suffused the house.

She stopped, her hand on the front door, wondering if she should tell them she was going out for a walk before breakfast. They would think it weird, ask all sorts of questions. She had to sneak out.

You should never leave the house without saying goodbye, without saying, *I love you*. It might be the last time you saw them. Olive had always said that, making every goodbye heavy with the threat of Fate.

Rachel opened the door and eased it shut behind her, creeping up the driveway alongside Dad's old car, and once out of sight, quickened her pace.

She'd answer their questions later.

— 44 —

A low winter sun had driven away the frost and fog, like a promise of new life. Arabella was standing before the church. Her bright smile warmed him right through and he forgot his headache.

'You look seedy,' she said, stroking a finger along his rough cheek.

They could walk out together now. She could take his arm. She was his betrothed. He should buy an engagement ring as a matter of urgency. Did one make an announcement in the newspaper?

'I only just remembered,' she said, 'that Reverend Colmore passed away five years ago. There's a new vicar here. Reverend Hopton.'

'Yes, of course.'

It was better like this. Colmore was to have performed her marriage ceremony, back then. She would not feel right looking him in the eye again. It was a failure visited on her. The sin that had been passed down to her by the man who had failed her.

They stepped into the church and he was grateful for the coolness and dimness of the interior.

The Reverend Charles E. Hopton seemed a rather austere young gentleman, not as warm and genial as he remembered

Reverend Colmore being.

They sat in the second row and the reverend perched on the end of the front row pew, turning back to them awkwardly, which seemed out of place for someone with his strict bearing.

Beadle raised the matter of their engagement and they discussed it tentatively, without committing to be wed there. The reverend made it clear that he would expect to see both of them a little more often on Sundays, even though they had made it clear they both attended other churches closer to their respective homes.

As they finished, Beadle turned and, as if an afterthought, said, 'Oh, perhaps you might help me with your opinion on a work related matter?'

The reverend looked at Arabella, as if she shouldn't be present.

'I have already discussed the matter with my wife to be,' Beadle smiled. 'She suggested I seek your opinion.'

'Of course, Inspector. How might I be of service?'

They strolled to the rear door of the church.

'A poison pen letter case which makes continued reference to Numbers 14:18.'

'Ah. The sins of the fathers.'

'Yes,' Arabella chimed in. 'When the Bible says the sins of the father will be visited upon the children, what does it mean? It seems rather unfair.'

'Numbers 14:18 is not the only mention of this,' the reverend smiled. 'It is also in Exodus 20:5. *You shall not bow down to them or serve them, for I the Lord your God am a jealous God, visiting the sins of the fathers on the children to the third and the fourth generation of those who hate me.*'

'Is God saying that the children and the grandchildren of the father would have to pay for the sins of their father?' Beadle asked.

'It's difficult for us to understand, but perhaps God

doesn't mean that at all, especially since Deuteronomy 24:16 says *Fathers shall not be put to death for their sons, nor shall sons be put to death for their fathers; everyone shall be put to death for his own sin.*'

'So what *is* God saying?' Arabella asked.

'My interpretation is that God is saying, if a father misleads his family, the family will pay for it. A sin, a mistake, can ripple through generations. Our base, selfish need for instantaneous gratification can have unforeseen consequences. In many ways, we all pay for the lack of foresight of previous generations. The strife we see all about us in these troubling times was forged by our fathers and grandfathers, and we have to wear the chains they forged.'

They came to the open door and the cool, green expanse of the graveyard.

'People think it rather callous of God to promise such retribution on people who are, in effect, quite innocent, but of course this rule is later overturned in the Book of Jeremiah.'

'There are contradictory laws in the Bible?' said Beadle, trying to smile.

'Just as in your line of work. It is up to the experts in law to argue the difference.'

'I hadn't thought of vicars as lawyers.'

'The original law was no longer having the intended effect.' Reverend Hopton allowed himself a smile. 'People thought only their descendants would be punished for their sins and they would get off scot free, you see?'

'I see,' said Beadle. 'If only our poison pen suspect was as aware of Jeremiah as he is of Numbers.'

'I shall make it the subject of tomorrow's sermon. Then perhaps he might see the error of his ways.'

They shook the vicar's hand and stepped out to the churchyard, just by Mr Rieper's fresh grave, the flowers already fading.

Beadle took out his pocket watch. 11.20.

He felt he had an appointment he'd forgotten, but he couldn't think of what it might be. Only that it filled him with dread.

— 45 —

Rachel walked across Moseley, through the village, already busy with its monthly farmers' market, and turned left down Chantry Road to Danny's student flat where she rang the bell. The front door opened and her heart sank to find Jessica standing there, a look of surprise on her face flitting from uncertainty to annoyance to haughtiness within a fluttering of her false eyelashes.

'Hi. Is Danny in?'

Jessica's look settled on her favourite expression when dealing with Rachel: examining something she'd just trodden in.

'He's in his room,' she said.

'I've got some research for him.' She indicated the file under her arm. The photograph of Amy and her father that she'd forgotten to give to Danny last night.

Jessica held out her hand. 'I'll see he gets it.'

Rachel gripped it more tightly under her arm. 'I need to talk to him about it.'

Jessica folded her arms and tried to look even more haughty, which was difficult, because she'd begun at such a high level of haughtiness there was almost nowhere else to go.

'Was he at yours the other night?' Jessica asked.

'What? No!'

Jessica looked her up and down, mentally totting up the price of her wardrobe. Rachel sighed at the tedium of it: this stupid, boring, rich girl who knew nothing and was of no importance to anyone and not a single person in the world would miss if she were to disappear this instant. And at the same time, she couldn't stop curling in on herself in shame.

Jessica stepped to one side and let her walk in, giving her a supercilious smile, as if she'd somehow taught her a lesson.

'It's upstairs. Second left.'

Rachel trudged up the stairs and knocked on his door. There was no answer. She knocked again. Nothing. She heard movement inside.

'Danny? It's Rachel. Danny? I'm coming in.'

She turned the handle and peered inside, hoping to God he wouldn't be naked or with a girl. And then the horrible thought that Amy Parker would be there with him. That he'd already gone and rescued her, removed her from 1912 and brought her here, where her mad father couldn't kill her.

He was lying in bed, asleep, and Amy Parker wasn't with him.

Rachel's eyes swept the wall above his desk. He had pinned up all of the documents they had researched like a police crime board: printouts of their library research; the death certificates; an enlargement of the photo he'd taken on his phone, her face ghostly and pixellated; a photo of the house as it was now, and as it was then, which he must have taken yesterday before coming back through.

She went to the bed and shook his shoulder. He jumped up, startled, blinking sleep from his eyes.

'Bloody hell! Oh, it's you.' His voice heavy with the weight of slumber.

'Snotty Cow let me in,' she said.

'Jessica?' he groaned, rubbing his face. 'She's all right.'

'If you like snotty cows. I've got another one for your shrine.'

'It's not a shrine,' he grumbled.

'I forgot to give it to you yesterday. The librarian found it for you.'

He took her file and opened it to see the portrait of Amy and her father. He gasped and then tried to cover it with a cough.

'It's a shrine,' she said. 'All it needs is a candle.'

'I'll ask Jess if she's got one,' he said. He reached for his iPhone, turning it over and swiping it. 'What the hell?'

His iPhone was dead.

'I forgot to charge it. Oh, God!' He sprang up like he'd been shot with an arrow, eyes bulging with shock.

'What?' she asked.

'The time!' he cried.

She fished her Nokia out of her pocket. 'It's 11.25.'

'No!' He leapt out of bed and tore off his vest.

Rachel turned away with alarm, staring out of the window. 'What are you doing?'

'Amy's going to die at 11.44! I can't believe this. Oversleeping. Phone dying.'

'Maybe fate is trying to stop you, Danny. Maybe it won't let you save her.'

'If she runs away with me, it can't happen. She can't die.'

Rachel turned. No, it was still not safe to look. He was half way through throwing on his Edwardian suit.

'Where are you going to take her?'

'I'll bring her back here if I have to.'

She turned and watched while he pulled his shirt over his torso. 'You'll probably kill her with the shock. Or she'll be the one going to Winson Green asylum.'

'Then I'll take her somewhere in her own time. We'll run away to London. Her father won't find us.'

He was almost completely Edwardian now.

Fury burned behind her eyes. 'Don't be ridiculous! You know you can't stop it!'

'I can do anything I like,' he said. 'Damn my stupid phone!'

She grabbed his lapels and he tried to shake her off, glaring like she was the crazy one. 'You've got to forget her!'

'I can't,' he said. 'I can't let him kill her.'

'I won't let you do this!'

'Try and stop me.'

He pushed her aside and headed out down the stairs, storming out of the front door, Rachel in his wake, trying to pull him back.

'Danny! You don't know what you're doing!'

'Just stay out of it, Rachel! It's none of your business!'

He ran off up the street and turned right, heading for the church. She watched him go, panicking, wondering what to do – frozen.

— 46 —

Beadle flapped his hat at his face, taking a draught of cool air. It had been so musty in there.

'Are you all right? You look pale.'

'I'm fine. The air in there was so stale.'

Arabella glanced over her shoulder, making sure they were out of earshot. 'And the sustenance also.'

'It all seems so irrelevant.'

'To think there are people filling their heads with such nonsense, and walking out to murder others, with God's words in their mouths.'

'You would not believe how often this is the case,' he said.

'Are you quite certain you are all right?' she asked, stroking his arm. 'You look so ashen.'

'I woke with a terrible head, but the fresh air will do me good.' He looked up at the church tower. The clock said 11.30. 'You said he used to come here. Was fascinated by a certain gravestone?'

'This way,' she said, leading him down the path.

A terrible sense of foreboding. There was something awful about today. He wished he could go to bed and start it all over again.

'Down there,' she said, pointing.

Dread seared his flesh.

'Is this a joke?' he groaned.

Arabella stepped away from him, alarm on her face. 'What is it?'

'That is my wife's grave.'

There, clear in the stone, a little green with moss. *Hermione Beadle (nee Calthorpe).*

'I'm to be buried there. Or I was.'

'I didn't know,' she said. 'I've never read the inscription. He would wander here and stare at it. I always watched him from there.' She pointed back to the rear door of the church.

Would he be buried here? It was written in his will. But the future he had set himself was all changed. Arabella was changing that future.

'What does this mean?' he said, faltering.

She rushed to his side, took his arm, holding him up. 'Come, let's go. I hate this place.'

He found his feet marching back up the path. Be careful not to fall flat on your face. They retreated, past Mr Rieper's grave, the church door, to walk around the church.

Arabella halted, pulled him back. 'Can we go the other way?'

'Why is that?'

'That corner,' she said. 'That spot right there. I've always been afraid to step there. It's always been as if someone has stepped on my grave. You think I'm silly.'

'Not at all,' he said, trying to laugh it off. 'We need never come here again. The place obviously holds too many bad memories for you.'

'But aren't we to be married here?'

'There are plenty of other places we can marry.'

They turned back down the path. He didn't want to walk past his wife's grave again, his own grave, but he would do it for Arabella. How strange, he'd talked to Hermione about her only this morning and now here he was right next to her body, with Arabella on his arm.

She halted again. 'No.'

'What is it?'

She shook her head, staring ahead in fear, as if a ghost blocked the path ahead. It was quite empty, but he wondered in an instant of panic if his dead wife had risen from the grave to block their way.

Arabella pointed to the gravestone. 'It's happening again.'

He couldn't see what was happening at all, and then arcs of blue lightning struck and tore the day open.

— 47 —

Rachel wondered if she should really stop him from saving a girl's life. Was that the right thing to do? He was already far ahead, in his Edwardian clothes, though he'd forgotten his hat. She thought wildly of running home to change into her tweed walking suit.

She ran full pelt down the parade of shops. Danny was on the other side running past the Fighting Cocks. Traffic blared through the village, cars and vans and buses. She ran till it thinned out and she could dart across to the green.

A quick glance up the alleyway.

Danny wasn't there. The gates were locked. He'd have gone round the long way. She stood frozen for a moment, wondering if she could climb the gates and beat him to the touchstone.

No, she crossed the sliproad and sprinted past the Bull's Head up St Mary's Row, her heart burning.

She ducked into the lychgate, knowing she was too late, tearing into the churchyard, over the buckled paving stone with the name *Arabella Palmer* and round the back of the church and down the path, breathless.

He wasn't there.

He'd gone through.

— 48 —

Beadle fell to his knee. It was as if a vengeful god had rent the curtain of day open. Arabella silent screamed, her fist to her mouth.

But it was not his dead wife come to exact revenge for his infidelity. It was Daniel Pearce. He appeared out of nowhere and then, as soon as he had appeared, he was running for the lower gate. He was through it before Beadle could stand.

'What on earth? Where did he come from?'

Arabella stared in wonder, frozen, like him.

It had been the man in the photograph, the Daniel Pearce that had haunted him for twenty-four years; the great white whale that had escaped. He had appeared in a flash of light and run without even seeing them.

'Come. We must give chase,' he shouted.

But it was his own legs that held them back, not Arabella's. What was it today? Something pressed on his soul, as if vice were slowly squeezing him to death.

Arabella moaned, and the air gathered in the same way it had just before Pearce had appeared, thickening like a swarm of wasps. It shimmered and burst like a blue balloon and a girl appeared.

— 49 —

Danny ran through the village, not noticing the wonders of a Saturday morning in 1912. He was thinking of how to get Amy away from her father. He glanced at the clock on the Fighting Cocks pub as he ran past.

11.35. Only ten minutes. No. Nine.

Could he persuade her to leave with him? What could he say? And where would they go?

He checked the wedge of 1912 money in his inside pocket. He could run away with her, get a train at New Street Station. Was it built already or would it be the old Curzon Street Station? No, New Street was a Victorian station; he'd seen photos of the old one with its amazing roof which had been damaged during the Blitz and then bulldozed in the sixties to make way for the new concrete monstrosity.

Sprinting past the Prince of Wales pub, he skirted a beggar who called out to him. He'd given him the coin, that first time. Calling out to him like an old friend.

They could run to New Street Station and buy a ticket to anywhere in the country, the coast, or maybe London, where they could disappear more easily.

He felt a thrill of expectation for all the things they might see, and then remembered the research he'd done into what happened in 1912. The world was still reeling from the sinking of the Titanic and a series of wars in the Balkans would explode into the First World War within a couple of years. It was like the entire world was sleepwalking into the abyss.

It was just about the worst time he could pick to be a young, able-bodied male.

No, he'd bring her back to the present with him.

Get her out of the house, walk to St Mary's, touch the stone, and disappear back to 2011.

Would it freak her out, like Rachel had said? Would she go insane at the sight of the modern world? Would it unhinge her as much as her father was unhinged?

He had no more time to think about it.

Six minutes.

He'd reached her house.

— 50 —

Rachel reached out to the touchstone and with an electric shock that buzzed in her teeth, she was back in the churchyard in an instant.

The rotting smell of the place gagged her as she gasped a deep breath and ran over soft grass to the wrought-iron gates at the back of the graveyard.

Stumbling down the slate slope, she heaved the gates open with all her strength.

Men loading barrels shouted as she ran past, heading for the chink of blazing light at the end of the alley that led to 1912.

* * *

'Stop!' Beadle cried.

The girl flinched, a criminal caught in the act, but she did not acknowledge his shout. She ran for the gate just like Pearce had. It creaked and groaned as she wrenched it open and fled.

'We have to stop them!' he said, though he had no idea what he was stopping.

They stumbled down the path and past his wife's grave. Pain shot through his ankle and he realized he was almost hopping, Arabella holding him up.

She heaved open the gate and they pushed through the wide-open space, dark behind the advertising hoardings, and stumbled for the slit of light at the end of the dark alley.

Bursting out onto the village green, he saw Joe locking his cabin and rushing to meet them.

'He just come again!'

'We know,' said Beadle. 'The girl too.'

'They've run that way.' Joe pointed north.

They could see the girl dashing up the street, already crossing the road at Shufflebotham's.

'They run too fast,' said Arabella.

'We know where they're going.'

'The Parker house,' said Joe.

* * *

Danny pulled up, bent over, chest burning, legs leaden. Should he just go to the front door and knock? There was no time to mess around. It could be happening right now.

A policeman walking towards him from Brighton Road. Could he tell him? Report the murder?

Or say he'd heard screams from inside so that he would knock the door? That alone might disrupt what was supposed to happen.

No. The police were after him. They had his name, knew he was after Amy Parker. This cop might be on watch, waiting for him to show. He'd be arrested and carted back to that cell. He couldn't help Amy from a police cell. She would be dead in the next five minutes.

He nipped down the side street, away from the policeman's gaze, and scooted round to the rear of the house.

He'd stopped thinking now and was all action: vaulting the fence, padding down the garden and climbing up to Amy's window, hoping no one from the houses all around would see him and alert the police. He didn't even know if they had telephones yet.

He raised himself slowly and peered into her bedroom through the open window.

He looked all around. It didn't matter if a neighbour saw him; he had to stop Parker killing his daughter.

He climbed into Amy's bedroom, his boot letting out an ear-splitting creak as he lowered it to the floor.

Suddenly, the door opened and he was caught.

— 51 —

They could never catch them. Beadle looked around wildly. The cabman's shelter sat behind them. 'There are no cabs!'

'Why don't we get the tram?' said Arabella. 'We can overtake them.'

They looked south to the dovecote. A tram sliding down the hill to the village.

'Yes, quickly!'

They ran across the green to the other side of the street, where Boots the chemist stood on the corner. A line of people already waiting.

The tram stopped at the crossroads and then slid slowly, gently to them. They piled on. The driver rang a bell and the tram pushed off, whirring and groaning as it climbed the hill.

They stood at the front, with a view of the entire street ahead.

'Move to the back,' the driver said. 'Take a seat.'

Beadle pulled his police identification from his pocket. 'Make lively. We're following a suspect.'

The driver's eyes bugged out of his head. 'I can't make it go any faster, officer.'

'Just get a move on!'

He gasped for air.

Arabella squeezed his hand on the steel railing.

He was too old for chasing criminals. He needed to retire on his pension and tend a garden with this beautiful woman.

They climbed the hill and stopped opposite the Prince of Wales to let a passenger on. Such agonising delay.

'Get a move on!' Joe shouted. 'This is police business!'

The tram whirred on, turning at the bend and began its descent down the gentle slope to Balsall Heath.

— 52 —

Danny stepped forward into the room, ready to fight Mr Parker.

But it was Amy.

She clamped her palm to her mouth, closed the door behind her and rushed to him.

He took her in his arms. She was trembling with fear.

'We can't talk today,' she whispered. 'My father's in a terrible mood. You have to go. If he catches you here…'

'Amy, you have to come with me, right now.'

'The police came for you. What have you done, Danny Pearce?'

'I told them your father was insane. That you were in great danger. But they wouldn't believe me.'

'My father wouldn't hurt me,' she said.

But he could see it in her face. It was the lie she desperately wanted to believe.

'He's hurt you already, hasn't he?'

She looked away, shaking her head from side to side, desperate not to see the truth.

'You know it,' he said. 'I'm here to save you.'

She sobbed, nodding and her face fell on his chest.

'We have to go. Now.'

She broke away, nodded and started to look around for

things to take with her, her hands shaking violently.

'We haven't time,' he said, glancing at a carriage clock on a shelf.

11.42.

'I'll need some things, though,' she pleaded.

'No, we need to go now, before he…'

Too late. Heavy footsteps clumping rapidly up the stairs. Her father's voice boomed out, 'Amy!'

She froze in terror.

Danny pulled her to the window, their only escape route. 'Come on!'

She couldn't move, staring at the door in terror. It flew open and Mr Parker was there.

'What's this?' he cried. 'Under my roof?'

Before either of them could move, he smacked Amy across the face with the back of his hand. She flew across the room and hit the wall, crumpling in terror. Danny stepped between them, arms out to protect. Mr Parker punched him square on the jaw. He reeled back, surprised. He hadn't felt it, but it had knocked him against the window.

'You whore! You vile whore! Abomination!'

'Father! Please! No! Stop!'

He loomed down over Amy and slapped her again across the face, her squeal of pain flaming inside Danny's head.

He dived at the old man. They crashed against the wardrobe.

Mr Parker slumped, dazed.

Danny grabbed Amy's hand and ran out of the door with her.

— 53 —

Beadle craned to see.

There. The girl, running desperately, one fist holding up her long skirt, dashing like a sprinter in a manner befitting no woman.

Ahead was the Parker house to the right, the tram depot beyond it, the tram stop opposite that on the left.

They caught up with the running girl and for a moment, Beadle's eyes met hers as she looked over her shoulder, flailing in wild panic.

'Oh God!' Arabella screamed.

Another girl, running into the road ahead. The Parker girl. She ran and stopped and looked behind her.

* * *

Rachel jumped as the tram let out a wail. She was so close now. It rattled alongside her, hissing, grumbling, taunting as it overtook, startled passengers watching her frantic sprint. She saw the house up ahead. Nearly there. And suddenly a bizarre scene erupted from it.

A girl ran out into the street. A young man came flying out of the house after her, as if fired from a cannon.

The tram's brakes screeched. Sparks flew up from the silver rails. The *ring-ring* of the tram bell split their ears.

* * *

Danny and Amy tore down the stairs, two at a time, stumbling, falling, flying, Mr Parker chasing them, Amy screaming hysterically.

On the lower landing, Parker jumped on Danny's back and they fell in a flailing, kicking heap.

Amy ran on down the stairs.

Danny booted Parker in the face, heard the sickening crack of his jaw as the old man flew back.

He jumped to his feet to follow Amy, saw Parker's face all red, flecks of spittle foaming at his mouth as he struggled back to his feet and stumbled after them.

He heard the whirr of the electric tram in the distance as he clattered across the tiles in the hall and bolted through the open front door behind Amy, who was rushing blindly down the garden path into the street.

And, as in a dream, he saw the tram looming and Amy running into its path.

She couldn't hear his disembodied cry.

Amy stood petrified in the street, staring in panic at her father, a monster spat from the house's mouth. She heard the tram's bell too late, twisted to see it almost upon her.

The brakes screeched, the bell rang, someone screamed. The driver slammed the brakes. Hit the bell.

They lurched forward. Arabella fell against him.

Beadle was pinned to the window, watching helpless as Amy Parker turned, frozen in horror.

* * *

An older man in a waistcoat dashed out of the house after the couple, waving a cane.

The girl stopped, wheeled around and saw the tram bearing down on her.

The young man careened across the street to catch her.

Rachel ran towards them, panic on her face, arm outstretched, too late, and shouted, 'Don't!'

* * *

Danny lunged and tackled Amy out of the tram's path.

It clattered by and hissed to a stop as Danny held her tight on the floor. He had a moment to realize they were alive, where he could feel her soft body under his, her breasts rising against him, panting, alive.

* * *

Rachel had a moment, before Parker slammed into her and pushed her to the floor, marauding across the street, waving a cane.

She fell and felt her knee scrape on the hard gravel road.

He'd saved her. Danny had been a blur, crashing in from the right to push Amy Parker out of the tram's path. There had been no crushing of bone, or the expected smash of steel on flesh.

* * *

The tram rolled on, brakes screeching, screams and cries of terror from the passengers. Beadle hammered at the door as the tram rolled to a slow stop, to hiss and splutter almost outside the tram depot.

'Open the bloody doors, man!'

'All right, all right,' the driver wheedled.

The door clattered open and Beadle jumped to the pavement. Arabella was beside him and they were running back up the street.

* * *

Danny jumped to his feet as Parker came screaming at them brandishing a cane.

'You whore! You vile whore! Abomination!'

Thwock!

He took the cane right across his face, stumbling to one side, blood spurting from his cheek.

Parker raised the cane again to strike Amy, then stuttered, confused, as the cane was snatched from his grasp and a crowd of passersby jumped on him and pinned him down.

A woman pulled Amy to the far kerb, wrapping her arms around her.

* * *

A crowd of people at the scene. More passersby running to them.

'Come on,' he cried. 'We have him.'

But Arabella was running faster than him. It was Beadle who was slowing them down. Such a terrible throbbing pain all down his left arm.

They ran up the street, along the tram tracks. A hansom cab clattered by and Arabella pulled him back. They might have died under the horse's hooves.

'Be careful, dearest,' she said.

For a moment, her tenderness took him by surprise and he wanted to stop and kiss her right there in broad daylight in the middle of the Alcester Road.

But he ran on, limping. Joe was behind, panting like an old dog.

* * *

Someone pulled Danny to his feet and dragged him away. He stared after Amy, dizzy, groggy, face bleeding, but triumphant, seeing Amy safe and her father still screaming biblical abuse at her from under a scrum of burly men.

'I did it,' he said. 'I stopped it.'

Amy stared back as he was dragged away from her. She understood it now. He caught her eyes for the last time and found himself yanked up into a pony trap.

Rachel was by his side and shouting at the driver, 'St Mary's church, please!'

The cabman whipped the horse off and they pulled away from the scene, speeding off up the hill to the village. Danny looked back in panic. Policemen were running to the scene.

'Come on,' said Rachel. 'You can't help her now!'

The pony trap rattled away.

Amy Parker was safe, a crowd of people gathering round her. Her face disappeared in the crowd.

Someone was laughing hysterically, laughing till they cried, and it wasn't until the carriage was pulling up at the village green that he realized it was him.

— 54 —

They arrived at the scene and Beadle pushed through the crowd, shouting, 'Police! Make way!'

He thought he only had to clamp his hand on Daniel Pearce, but found the girl, Amy Parker, moaning and crying, hysterical, being held by a woman.

Her father, Mr Parker, was spitting hate, held down by three men. A constable ran up. Women gasped outrage at Parker's stream of obscenities.

He looked around for Pearce, but he was nowhere.

'There!' cried Arabella, pointing up the road.

A hansom cab – the same cab that had almost run him over – darting away up the rise back to Moseley. Daniel Pearce looking back at the scene.

'Constable. You take charge here.'

Another cab coming from Balsall Heath, empty, the driver wary of the crowd in the street.

'Make way!' Beadle screamed.

He flagged the driver through the parting crowd. The men dragged Richard Parker to the opposite side of the street to his daughter. Beadle leapt into the cab. Arabella jumped up beside him.

'Police!' he called. 'Follow that cab up ahead! Catch him if you can!'

The driver cracked his whip and they cantered from the scene.

'We have to catch him,' he cried. 'It's him. I know it!'

Arabella stroked his fists with her cool, soft hands, and he relented a little, breathing deep.

Joe was somewhere behind, at the scene, no doubt telling the constable he was a police deputy.

They clattered up the rise and crested the hill around the bend and as Moseley village came into view below, he saw Pearce's cab pull up alongside the green.

'Faster, man!'

The cabbie whipped his horse on and they thundered down the hill. Pearce and the girl jumped from their cab and ran into the alley by the giant Oxo hoarding.

They pulled alongside the empty cab and Arabella leapt out, Beadle jumped down beside her, a jolt of searing pain through his knees, and they were running up the dark alley to the wrought-iron gates.

He could see them, at his wife's grave. The girl looked back in panic. A flash of blue light as from a photographer's flashbulb. It seared his eyeball and floated in his sight as they pushed through the gate.

He ran to his wife's grave, panting like a dying dog. They were gone.

He fell to his knees, one hand slamming against the gravestone. His wife's name there, accusing. And his name too. *Loving wife of Wm. Beadle.*

Arabella crouched beside him and seemed more concerned with him than the disappearance of Pearce.

'No one can disappear into thin air like that.'

Someone was moaning in pain. Arabella stroked his face, her eyes livid with fear. She seemed to be saying with her eyes that they both knew that wasn't true. He remembered the drawing she had shown him from Pearce's sketchbook. Daniel Pearce pointing a gun on a station platform, under a clock, fading from view. He remembered the eagle feather he kept in the journal in the drawer at work.

Pearce was gone again. The great white whale had escaped into the ocean's depths.

Someone was moaning, and Arabella was stroking his face.

He felt himself fading, just like the man in the drawing.

Such a colossal pain in his arm, and across his chest. And he knew, in that final moment before his heart gave out, that this was the end. The future he had mapped out with Arabella was not to be.

He read his wife's name again on the stone, and below it his own.

Loving wife of Wm. Beadle.

He sought Arabella's beautiful blue eyes weeping for him, and he sank into darkness.

— 55 —

When she came through and felt the rush of now hit her, Danny was lying on the grass, shouting up at the sky. 'I did it! I did it! Get in!'

He jumped to his feet and wheeled around, punching the air, the adrenalin that had erupted inside him with the fight still sizzling in his veins, blood smeared down his cheek.

Rachel steadied herself, feeling a rush of dizziness. 'Promise me we never go back again,' she said. 'It's too dangerous.'

'What are you worried about?' Danny cried. 'It all turned out fine, didn't it?'

She dug out his bag from under the bush and threw it at him. He caught it, still grinning infuriatingly. She reached out to him and brushed his cheek, blood on her fingertips. He winced away from her.

'You should get that seen to. It looks nasty. He could have killed you.'

'He could have killed *her*. I stopped it. She's going to live. I wonder how long for?'

'We'll see in the library,' she said. 'Maybe she died the next day.'

'You're a real glass half full girl, aren't you? We changed history!'

They staggered up the path, both breathing heavily, taking unsteady steps, and walked out onto St Mary's Row through the lychgate: busy, overcast, Saturday afternoon St Mary's Row in the year 2011, all normal, just as they'd left it this morning. She turned to him.

'You'll get that seen to, won't you?'

'Don't worry about me,' he said.

He was already marching down the slope to the village, an absurd spring in his step. He was so full of himself.

He wheeled around and called to her, laughing. 'Rachel! Thank you! Thank you for helping me!'

She turned and trudged up Wake Green Road, walking the half a mile to home, piecing it together, wondering what might have happened to them all. Had Mr Parker died in the asylum just as he had before or was it murdering his own daughter that had done that to him? No, it was the syphilis that had killed him. His date with the asylum was assured and they were probably carting him off there right now. Had Amy survived and grown to be a woman, and if so, when had she finally died? And if they'd changed that, made her live longer, maybe have children herself, what effect would her life, branching out, have on other lives around her?

She clumped up her garden path, so exhausted that she didn't notice the new car in the drive. She put her key in the door and turned it. It stuck. Something was wrong. She rattled it a few times but it wouldn't click the Yale lock open. She sighed and pressed the doorbell and listened as someone approached inside. Olive opened the door.

'My key's not working,' she said, stepping inside. 'We'll have to get—'

Olive shoved her back. 'Hey! What's going on?'

Rachel stumbled back onto the drive. 'What's wrong? It's me, Nan. Rachel.'

Olive looked scared. 'Martyn! Someone's trying to come in!'

'Nan! Are you all right? Don't you recognize me?'

Martyn rushed to Olive's side and stepped in front of her. He'd dressed up for something; he looked all smart and clean but there was anger in his eyes. What was happening?

'What's wrong with Nan, Dad?'

'Hey, bugger off!' he shouted. 'I don't know what funny game you think it is but take it somewhere else!'

'Dad!' she cried.

'I'm not your bloody Dad. Go on! Sling it, you bloody druggie!'

She saw this was no joke, she saw it in the menace in his eyes, and yes, the fear too. She backed away and felt herself crumpling up like a sheet of paper burning, everything she knew melting from under her, the horror dawning on her.

'No,' she moaned. 'This isn't happening. No. No. No.'

'Go on!' Martyn shouted. 'Now! I'm calling the police!'

Tears were already falling down her face as she silently screamed and broke into a run.

She ran crying down Wake Green Road and through the village and down Chantry Road and was hammering at Danny's front door with her fists, shouting his name.

The door flung open and he lurched back as her fists hit him.

'What the hell are you doing?!' he shouted.

She grabbed hold of him. 'Danny. Does anyone recognize you?'

'What?'

'My Dad and my Nan. They don't know me!'

'What do you mean?'

'Something's happened!' she screamed. 'They don't know who I am! I don't exist!'

Jessica pushed her way to the front door, shouting 'What the bloody hell's going on?' She looked Rachel up and down with disgust. 'Oh my god, it's not some gypo woman selling pegs is it? Tell her to bugger off, whoever she is!'

She flounced back inside. Danny stared in shock.

'What's happened?' whimpered Rachel.

'I don't know,' he said.

She slapped him right on his bleeding cheek. 'What have you done! What have you done!'

'I don't know!'

'It's her. She's changed it all. You stopped her dying, and now I don't exist. It's *her!*'

She backed away down the path, a sudden gleam of venom in her eyes.

'What do you mean?' said Danny.

'She was supposed to die, Danny!'

She ran off up the street. There was only one place to go. The touchstone.

— EPILOGUE —

She reached the gravestone, heart pounding, doubled over, wheezing for breath. She looked all around to check she was alone and reached out to touch the spot.

Her fingers burned and the lights went out. There was a roaring in her ears. She stumbled around, blind, tripping over a mound in the grass, falling to her knees. The roaring sound became an eerie drone and an insane wailing. She blinked at the darkness and peered up at the sky. A sudden beam of light flashed across the blackness and she saw that she was still in the churchyard but it was night. She stumbled to her feet and gazed up in awe.

The droning sound that split her ears came from the dark, brooding sky, across which evil shapes flew – so many – lit by searchlights. The wailing sound was an air raid siren. There was a continual *crump-crump-crump* of Ack-Ack guns, and somewhere beyond the village the *ding-ling-ling* of fire engines in the distance. The searchlights knifed the blackness and the red glow of a hundred fires lit up the great barrage balloons floating above the city.

Rachel reeled with shock, dizzy, unable to take it all in. The noise of explosions nearby was deafening, bombs falling dangerously close and closer.

'Rachel!'

She wheeled round, trying to locate the voice. A man was standing at the wrought-iron gate. He was wearing a military cap with a trench coat.

She stared, dumbfounded.

He seemed surprised that she didn't recognize him. He must have thought it was the uniform because he swiped his hat off.

But she knew she'd never seen him before.

'Rachel! It's *me*, Charlie!' he shouted. 'You told me to meet you here, remember?'

She wanted to respond but her lips wouldn't move. She could only gawk, paralysed.

There was a sudden ear-splitting whistle of a bomb falling overhead. The soldier looked up in panic. She remembered he seemed to have a kind face and wondered if he was an angel. It screamed down on them and there was a moment of peace when she knew she was going to die, before the whistle erupted in an almighty explosion and the world turned black.

Thank you…

… for buying and reading *The Sins of the Fathers*.

If you liked it, please take a minute or two to give it a short review where you bought it. You won't be seeing adverts for Touchstone books on billboards or station platforms, but a simple review can be just as effective to an independent author like me.

Look for announcements on all Touchstone books at andyconway.net

Next in the Touchstone saga

Family at War

Dealing with the catastrophic fallout of their previous encounter with Amy Parker in 1912, Rachel now finds herself pitted against Danny during the Blitz.

FREE DOWNLOAD

A chilling investigation into the truth behind the Touchstone series...

"A cracking, spooky short story which is a real head-wrecker..."

Jack Turner, author *Valentine's Day*

amazon kindle nook kobo iBooks
Windows android BlackBerry

Sign up for Andy Conway's New Releases mailing list at www.andyconway.net and get a free copy of The Reluctant Time Traveller.

Also by Andy Conway

Touchstone Season One eBook Box Set

This Ebook Box Set edition contains all six novels in Touchstone Season 1, comprising over a quarter of a million words, and 1000 pages in the original paperback editions. Over the course of six adventures, and an entire century of local history, *Touchstone Season 1* builds into a moving coming-of-age saga that has won plaudits from young and old readers alike with its intelligent blend of time travel adventure, science fiction, historical romance and fantasy.

"I believe it's one of the best series of its kind."
"Had me hooked from start to finish... It's a magnificent story."

"If you haven't read this series yet — you simply must! But beware — you will be hooked!!"

"So good has got into my dreams and is only surpassed by Jack Finney the master in time travel, but if this guy carries on in same vein I cannot wait…"

Buried in Time

The Touchstone series of time travel historical adventures continues with this stand-alone opener to the second season, a Victorian suspense thriller dripping with mystery and horror.

July, 1888. Two months before Jack the Ripper's Whitechapel murders begin, a killer stalks the streets of Victorian Birmingham, the heart of England's industrial revolution.

"Inventively brilliant alternative history... deeper, darker and more inventive."

"A brilliant book again from Andy Conway."

"Great read, and thought provoking on whom Jack the Ripper really was."

Bright Star Falling

The time travel saga goes into the West... When a mysterious redhead plunges from the sky onto the Montana plains in 1874, she is taken in by Sitting Bull's tribe and named Bright Star Falling.

Torn between dark dreams of the past and bloody visions of the future, might she be the spirit whose re-appearance spells the end of the Lakota people?

"I have been waiting for the release of the eighth novel in the Touchstone series and this fabulous book definitely did not disappoint. It immerses the reader in the fascinating and tragic world of the Native Americans whilst still keeping the Touchstone theme. A brilliant and enjoyable read, I couldn't put it down!"

"Fantastic story. A world away from the Birmingham of season one but the Wild West and time travel – what a brilliant combination."

Bright Star Rising

Buffalo Bill visits Birmingham, and in his Wild West entourage is an amnesiac white woman who has lived with the Lakota Indians for over a decade.

Her name is Katherine Bright Star Falling. And she thinks she might have come home.

But the city's lawless police force, a zealous Pinkerton agent, and Birmingham's notorious cutthroat gang, the Peaky Blinders, will stop at nothing to claim the price on her head.

Weaving an alternate reality around Buffalo Bill's historic trip to Britain, *Bright Star Rising* blends fact and fantasy in this latest thrilling instalment of the Touchstone time travel saga.

Crossing over into the Touchstone universe (specifically *Touchstone 5: Let's Fall in Love for the Last Time*), this timeslip ghost story is a moving, evocative meditation on love and betrayal and the persistence of memory.

The Very Thought of You is a novella about a young man's obsession with Amy, the dead wife of an old man he visits. Community visitor Jez is assigned Harold, a cantankerous old codger who takes a venomous delight in confrontation and lives in a house that is falling down around him. But when Jez starts to see Amy's ghost and finds himself propelled into the house's secret past, his obsession with her threatens his hold on the present.

"Suspense, mystery, intrigue and supernatural... this delivers on all aspects... Couldn't put it down! Finished it in almost one sitting."

GHOSTS ON THE MOOR
ANDY CONWAY

Three women spend Christmas in a remote cottage on Dartmoor to escape problems at home, but their long hike across the moor turns tragic as old ghosts return for vengeance…

"Dartmoor at Christmastime. What a spine-tinglingly perfect setting for a ghost story. The three women with a complicated past could take the book into a dreary (for me) chicklit direction, but it actually gives the ghost story its bite. It might arguably be described as a present-day M.R. James as thoroughly malevolent ghosts wreak havoc on our heroines... It's a cracking little ghost story."

"Glad I read this in the morning — at least I got my sleep in first. I shall think twice about going to Devon again."

Printed in Great Britain
by Amazon